Through the Eye of Old Man Kyle

Through the Eye of Old Man Kyle

A Novel

PETER BILES

RESOURCE *Publications* · Eugene, Oregon

THROUGH THE EYE OF OLD MAN KYLE
A Novel

Resource Publications
An Imprint of Wipf and Stock Publishers
199 W. 8th Ave., Suite 3
Eugene, OR 97401

www.wipfandstock.com

PAPERBACK ISBN: 979-8-3852-2077-9
HARDCOVER ISBN: 979-8-3852-2078-6
EBOOK ISBN: 979-8-3852-2079-3

September 1st, 2017, 11:19 A.M.

Dear Professor Snodgrass,

Again, thank you for agreeing to take my creative writing project at the end of the summer after my several lame attempts to generate something this spring. You were asking for a "documentary view" of a memorable experience I've had, and while maybe it was a bit presumptuous to figure the most memorable experience was yet to come, I'm glad you gave me the three months of wiggle room. Because it turns out I was right.

You said at the beginning of the spring semester that telling a good story was about getting into someone else's shoes, trying out the world from their point of view, and seeing how it fares with your own. We read To Kill a Mockingbird *to get that through in our heads. You additionally said it was your hope for the class that we'd learn that kind of imaginative "skillset" by the end of the semester.*

I'd like to say I learned to imagine life from the eyes of another human being, and could tell you that the best stories help us do just that. But maybe there was further purpose in delaying my final project, because I can safely say that before this summer I have never really been challenged to walk a mile in another dude's boots. Maybe I thought it was supposed to be easy—this shift in viewpoint. Or that getting inside another person's mind wouldn't change how I saw things.

As you'll see in the following pages within my summer documentary of Camp Woodward, where I've worked every summer for the past four summers, I had a chance to get clubbed over the head with the fact that I'm an imagination novice, that while I learned a lot at Winston's College and am proud of my Bachelor's in the Biological Sciences, I still got a long way to go in the journey. About half of this account was written as the events unfolded, in a journal, and then I went back and combed it over after the summer to add all the stuff I didn't have time to write in the moment. Or rather all the stuff that only really accumulated after I had a chance to mull it over a couple of weeks. Maybe that's sort of like life? Half direct experience, and half reflection on direct experience? Or maybe the ratio is skewed way in favor of the latter. I don't know.

Really what follows, Professor, is all about my trying to get back in touch with this odd experience I had at the very beginning of my last summer at

Camp Woodward. There's much more to it, but at the end of the day, I wanted to feel like there really is a Watchman beyond the stars. Like there's a whole other world to be seen through the eye of Old Man Kyle, our local camp legend. Maybe by the time you reach the end, you'll sort of get what I mean.

All the best,

Hunter Saint

May 24th

Here goes, Prof: Once upon a time there was a camp of tin buildings atop a hill overlooking a lake in the outback woods of southeastern Oklahoma. I worked at that camp for four summers in a row, counting this one. Call it an emporium of hard work. Call it a play place for church kids who don't have good home lives. I call it home and highwater—and here's why.

It feels weird, but refreshingly familiar, being back. Like taking a deep breath after you've been holding it for a couple of minutes. I honestly don't even know if I've fully processed graduation. They flew us through commencement, as you know. You and I barely got to shake hands. We walked across the stage in tassels and robes and honors. Did I botch the handshake with President Clerk? There's no way to remember. The last two weeks have been a blur of moving cabinets and unruly laundry, of congratulatory cards from relatives I never see, and the feeling of another commencement into something new, whatever that newness entails. All that cliché talk you told us to avoid, Prof.

My sister, the lovely Carey Saint Morgan, got married, and I was in the wedding. That was the Saturday after graduation. She and Jared are happy so far as I can tell and are spending the next couple weeks in Costa Rica.

But now here I am at Camp Woodward, established in 1987, hereby in its thirty first year of operations, working here for the fourth year in a row. It's the home away from home where I can safely say that that other world of final exams, lack of sleep, cars, emails, and romantic confusion is pretty much removed. Well, maybe not the romantic confusion. Sometimes that element intensifies here by about a thousand degrees. But we'll get into that later. Here, it's quiet. Not quiet as in lack of noise, per say, since there are plenty of cicadas, locusts, and bird calls to madden the air, but quiet in terms of spiritual respite. That's how I see it, anyway. Camp Woodward is not *mechanical*. No engines or ringing phones or hissing espresso machines or rumbling generators. Some staffers say it's a bubble, totally disconnected from the "real world," as if this place requires a suspension of belief to enjoy.

That never seemed quite right, though. After every summer, I'd go back to college in the fall, quickly get thrown back into the melee of duties and lab assignments and the occasional wonderment over why I'm doing any of this, and then in May find myself back on this dock and dipping my toes in the healing waters of Lake Woodward. By all accounts *this* is the real world. The Shawnee hills roll in the distance like green putty. Tart blue skies, sprayed with stratus clouds, mark the beginning of a hot summer. The hills and the skies and the trees and the resident beasts of the surrounding forestry are still here, like they're supposed to, and invite the human invaders to partake in the contentment.

I'm sitting on the dock with my feet in the water, thighs against the edge so it feels like I could fall in at any moment. A huge catfish bellied in the mud when I first got down here. He was stirring up muck, only to flit off when my shadow crossed him. Now there's just perch bickering in the reeds and a water moccasin coiled in the grass underneath the water jug.

I really don't know why I decided to buy a *hardcover* journal. I'll have to transcribe all of this into a computer document at the end of the summer anyway, I guess. My deadline is September 1st or I don't officially pass college, which would be awkward since my diploma is setting on my dresser at home. It's not even a journal. More like a sketchbook. I'm writing tiny. I feel like a monk hunched over some ancient manuscript, translating Latin into Old English, or whatever. I've never kept a journal in the introspective sense or tried to document a section of life like this. But now that college is over and I have to actually start thinking about what to do with the rest of my life, it's as good a time as any to try and figure some things out on the page. I've heard writing down your thoughts is good for you, anyway. It helps you construct your life into a story. Helps you make at least some minimal sense of things and abide by the insights. Professor Snodgrass, you'd agree, no? Or is it the other way around? Is writing about trying to figure out the story that's already been presented to you? Huh. In any case, I'm already thinking about things that I otherwise would have. Maybe because I always knew, up until this summer at least, that the gentle shores of Camp Woodward would always be waiting to host me for a chunky three months of respite, so I didn't feel the need to jot things down to remember any of it. I felt like my time at Camp Woodward was never going to end.

Tonight, we've got orientation, and all the formality. It's always a giddy, nervous time for the newcomers, and an old hat for veterans like me to don with well-earned authority. Zach and I'll sit in the back next to Gabe the old maintenance guy and his young protégé, Jerry. But orientation is when Jenni really comes out full flare. She intimidated me during my first summer here, to be honest. She's this sharp-eyed thirty-year-old gal in a blue blazer, chewing gum under a ball cap, ponytail bouncing all over the place. I remember she perched up on stage with her clipboard, and she asked me if I had a highlighter. I mean, who has a highlighter on them at random? Funny thing, though, I did have one. It was in the pen pocket in my backpack, and after I handed it to her, she made some lines with it and then set it next to her leg on the stage in the cafeteria. I considered it a real act of courage just asking for it back.

Jenni has worked at Camp Woodward in some form or another for fourteen years, ever since she was in high school. She grew up in Adler, which is where I'm from, too, and started coming out to camp in the summers with her father. Her dad used to preach to some of the churches that came through. When Jenni was sixteen, she signed on for a two-week internship, wowing the administration with her quick judgment, no nonsense obedience, and voracious appetite for fun, and was offered a seat on the council not long after she graduated high school a year later. She's never looked back, and she's never gotten married.

Now Jenni treats me like a cousin. Or a nephew. Sometimes like an old son. When I go off to college, we always keep up a texting thread, and she'll FaceTime when she's walking from the camp office to her own house, which is just behind the rec field and overlooking the rest of the property like a resident temple. All said and done she's been the best boss I've ever had, and one of the best friends, too.

Here comes Lorrie, in the present tense.

She's coming down the hill towards the dock, arms swinging, looking down at me through her sunglasses. She's probably wondering what the heck is Hunter Saint doing on the dock scribbling in a journal. Maybe she'll think it's romantic and poetic. This is me making up for the fact that I was a biology major. Actually, it's just me making up for an assignment.

We'll see.

May 25th

Jenni said I wasn't going to make entries every single day, even if it is for a class assignment (because we all know what a fantastic and diligent student I am). Not a chance. She said we were too busy here to think and reflect deeply on the nature of the universe. I told her that I never said that was the goal. It's for an assignment. My last assignment of my college career. She's kidding, of course. But also, kind of not kidding. I can see where she's coming from with that. We average six and a half hours of sleep a night here at Camp Woodward.

But here we are. Day two.

It's five in the morning, and still mostly dark. The locusts are chattering, and it's going to be a clear day. I can see a few wisps of clouds above the trees. They look like chalk scrapes against a blackboard. The canoes are laying on their sides up against some bushes at the cusp of the woods, covered with clumps of dirt and cobwebs from a year of stationary repose. I always wanted to come out here in the winter and take one of the boats out, but never really got around to it. Now it was probably home to a band of copperheads, fire ants, and brown recluses. Gotta love Oklahoma's aboriginal underworld. Camp Woodward is always teeming with horrifying glories.

So maybe from now on this whole journaling enterprise will be a way I prove Jenni wrong. I know for a fact I can write in it every day. At least a little bit. It's not like I have to write a novel in here each morning. Just a quick review of yesterday and a prequel for what's coming. That's all I want—a record to remember my last summer at Camp Woodward.

Lorrie came down to the dock yesterday. I thought maybe she wanted to swim, but she had her Bible with her, and *Mere Christianity* by C.S. Lewis stacked on top of it. She said hello to me, and I perked up and said hey back, cheerfully and with my usual smile, asked her how the school year was. She had just graduated from Oklahoma City University as a Comm major. That's "communication," not "communism," just so we're clear. I tried to remember the last time we actually talked. It must have been at the Christmas party. Up until November we would text almost daily and call every week or so. And then after the party we just stopped. I can't say why exactly. I guess we just ran out of things to talk about, and I don't remember who initiated the distance. We exchanged greetings at the party and then spent the night catching each other staring the whole night through as we talked to other people. Jenni said the ogling was obvious and asked me why we didn't have a conversation like normal people. "I don't know," I said. "I want to. I always want to."

It's so easy to feel "close" to somebody when all you're doing is texting them, but five minutes of actual proximity makes you realize how illusory all that is. It's easy to text. Safe. A highly controlled environment. Here there's no buffer to keep us so closely apart, so intimately removed from our actual lives. Here there are no phones.

I guess that's why I was kind of surprised that she *did* make it all the way to the dock. She didn't veer to the waterfront and pretend to get something from the lifeguard shack. She didn't zipline into the deep end of the lagoon and dry off and go right back up to the cafeteria. She came down and she sat down on the dock next to me and said hello—the actual word "hello," not "hey," or "hi."

She asked me how it felt to be graduated, and I said it felt pretty good, but weird, that it had gone by so fast, yada yada, and that I was glad to be back at camp at least, and no, I didn't know what I was doing in the fall. "That must be nice," she said, and bent her head so her dark brown hair fell past her face. Then she asked me if I ever came down to the lake at night to look at the stars. That's the problem with breaking the ice once you've been apart for so long. Getting past the awkward niceties that don't mean anything. But you have to do it. You really do.

I replied that yes, on occasion. After busy days when I need to recharge and refocus. And then she kept talking about how she had never been to any place on earth that had so many stars. On the college campus, they were mostly blotted out by light pollution. Here, the only thing distracting from the stars was the flame from an oil refinery, heralding its light over the rolling hills like a mimicry of God's pillar of fire in the wilderness.

I asked her if she was doing okay, and she said, after a shrug and a half smile, she was "working through some things." To that, I didn't really know what to say. She's always been sort of a mystery. Like sometimes she's on top of the world and ready to kiss me and then others like she just wants to curl into a little ball and sink into the lake. Yesterday it felt like she was in between those two worlds, trying to figure out which one to fall into. I could tell she wanted to talk to me. About what exactly, I didn't know.

I told her that if she needed someone to talk to, she could talk to me, and she smiled and nodded, said okay, thanks, "I will."

It's a bit lighter now. The first breeze is sending some ripples across the lake, and the last of the stars are burning out against a pale blue backdrop of sky. Maybe it isn't so hard to be poetic.

It's all in how hard you look at things, and how hard they look at you back.

May 26th

It's probably time I write about Jordan.

There are usually a couple of off-color types who come and work at Camp Woodward. There are always anomalies. Everyone here is kind of weird in their own way, of course. You have to be kind of an oddball to come to a camp in the middle of nowhere to work sixteen hours a day seven days a week and report shiningly on the experience thereafter, while other college kids report their three months of well-earned cash from working internships in air-conditioned offices. But anyway. Most people who work here are pretty easy to get along with and talk to, but every year there's one or two who stick out or need more time to adjust than the others. This year it's young Jordan.

During orientation, two days ago now, he sat alone in a chair three rows removed from the rest of the Woodward disciples, manspread legs and unlaced shoes and greasy hair presenting him as this summer's resident prodigal. Jenni told me she received Jordan's application via his principal at Adler High School, who purportedly explained that though Jordan didn't go to church and wasn't necessarily known for his Christian values and character, he would "benefit greatly" from being immersed in a great environment like Camp Woodward.

He wore dark clothes, and his jaw worked a lot, and I originally figured that, okay, him working at Camp Woodward was sort of like his summer of reform. Maybe he'd done something, gotten expelled, and toiling at a summer camp was part of his community service agreement. Jenni believed in second chances. She was the best kind of American. And of course, she was sincere on the grace of God. She couldn't get enough of the grace of God. So, Jordan is among us, a fellow disciple, one of the twelve. He's young, just eighteen, and has no plans for college. I couldn't find him on social media.

I didn't talk to him at orientation. I'm not even sure he was there the entire time—another no-no in Jenni's book.

After we did intros, got through the icebreakers, which involved punting a beach ball covered with questions to each other while standing in circle, and signed our tax stuff, Jenni pulled me aside by the coffee maker in the cafeteria, looking over my shoulder. "I got a favor to ask," she said.

"What's up?"

"This kid Jordan."

"Uh-huh."

"He's a kid. A child. He barely knows where he's at, or what continent he's on."

"So why'd he come here?"

"His school sent him here. Or strongly encouraged him to apply. That's what he said in his application anyway. They figured that he'd be all right here because he won't have a lot of time to himself."

"Okay."

"He's depressed, Hunter—that's what I'm trying to say. Borderline suicidal. We've had depressed staff before, but not like this. He's a new beast."

"You were good to include him in the group," I said.

"Sure. I want to help him. But I'm just connecting with you, Zach, and Lorrie mainly to see if you could maybe make it a point to, like, talk to him, make sure he's doing okay. Especially when the first group of kids comes through and he has to actually do stuff."

"Sure. I can do that," I said.

She smiled, leaning her head back and patting my shoulder. "You're the best."

I'm pretty good at talking to people. At least, I never had a problem with that sort of thing. I don't think I'm really a full-blown extrovert and was kind of low key a lot in college, but here, I feel like Zach and I are the alpha dogs, meritorious of respect. Everyone likes us here. We're the go to dudes when there's a snake in the dorm lobby or a toilet's overflowing. But we don't want to strut around and bark at people. We're the *chill* alpha dogs this summer—the guys who are pals with Jenni and know all the past pranks and have access to all the secret nooks and crannies of the camp. This being our fourth and final year, we've earned the privilege of being Camp Woodward's laid-back insiders. I told Zach about Jenni's request, and he nodded, saying how she had texted him something along those lines a few days ago. "Honestly man, I can kind of tell when they're going to quit," he told me. "You know how it goes. Every year there's at least one person who throws in the towel. He may not even be here tomorrow."

After he said that, I was about to go over and talk to Jordan, just to introduce myself, but when I stood from the folding chair and started to head over, something about the way he was slouching back, arms crossed, and tapping his foot against the concrete with his gray eyes trained out the window, made me stop and pretend to get a cup of coffee from the bar.

Zach chuckled at my reroute, but he didn't end up going over to Jordan either. He checked his phone, and I checked my phone. We'll have to turn those in later tonight. After that we will have to twiddle our thumbs or pray for escape in situations like those.

I think meeting Jordan will happen naturally. You can't always force this kind of stuff. Maybe the word is "organic." Can't force a tree to grow. We're going to run into each other on the way to breakfast and strike up a conversation about punk rock, which I listen to from time to time, and all my guilty assumptions about him being a dark-minded junkie are going to yield a fresh and complicated picture of a young man who's just searching for God in all the wrong places. I'm not going to force anything on him. Maybe with that approach, along with the likewise coordination of my peers, he might end up coming to *us*.

He set up his bunkbed in the corner of the dorm room. This year there's only five guys working at camp, and seven girls. Small staff this year. Zach and I glanced at him before going to bed. We always take the other corner of the room, this little nook. Jordan sat stooped over on the edge of his bed with his ankle on his knee, scrolling through his phone, almost sliding off the slick mattress. I don't think anyone has heard him talk yet. He'd wrapped black blankets all around the bed. Then he ducked under his curtains, turned on a box fan, and that was that. No one told him that he wasn't supposed to have his smartphone on him anymore. But honestly it doesn't even matter. There's no service here, anyway. Also, I think that stripping him of his single source of interest and investment might backfire on us. Jenni has most likely already thought all of this through.

James and Rory, the twenty-year-old twins who somehow caught wind of Camp Woodward all the way up from Duluth, Minnesota, came in around 1 a.m. after playing basketball, huffing with exhaustion and debriefing their play in whispers. I was still awake, staring into the darkness above me. The twins activated the flashlights on their phones, stumbling over the recliner and kicking the old communal guitar on so it jangled with a badly tuned hum. Even after they finally went to bed, I didn't get much sleep. I listened to Jordan's box fan across the room. The white noise was comforting, in a way. At camp, it usually doesn't matter what foibles you formerly used to fall asleep. Here, you don't need anything but your own hard worked weariness to conk out, and that's a greatly rewarding feeling—hard work, hard rest. But no, I didn't get much sleep, even so.

This morning we're going to paint the green wall by the waterfront. Every summer before the first camp rolls in their big school buses at the end of May, we paint it, and after every year, the wall peels and distributes itself with equanimity into the crab grass. I keep telling Jenni she ought to get some more weatherproof paint. But it's almost like we have an infinite store of preexisting paint that's been around since the eighties or something, and it would injure the economy of scarcity to reject the motherload. It's all right. Gives us something to do today on the last day before a free day. Shoot. The day after that, a church from Edmond comes and then after that it's one camp after the next! All summer long.

May 27th

Warm morning. About eighty degrees and humid as heck. They say it's going to be a wet first half of the summer, and then a dry second half.

Got up a little later than planned today. I like to be the first one out of bed, for some reason. Like I have the drop on everyone else. I'm journaling in the cafeteria today because it started to rain, and apparently we're getting tornado watches this afternoon. I checked my phone last night in Jenni's office and found out that I didn't get the internship for the fall at Reming Labs in the city. Still waiting for the letters from OU Med and Johns Hopkins. Haha. Like the latter would ever happen…I just sent it on a whim. Although you can't whimsically apply to medical school. I had to bust my butt.

Speaking of phones, here's a story. Yesterday, Jenni paired me and Jordan up together to paint the wall by the waterfront. She was strategic. I hadn't talked to him yet, and I promised her I would when the "opportunity" arose. At first I felt, I don't know, miffed or something? Like she'd already given up hope of my talking to him on my own initiative. I mean, we've only been here like two days. But I get it. She doesn't want this kid to leave prematurely. Like Zach said, that's happened in the past.

Anyway, we walked down the sandy road with our paint buckets, me in my crocs, running shorts, and staff shirt and Jordan in his black pants, converse shoes, and droopy gray hoodie. It was already ninety degrees by the time we'd been assigned our jobs. "You're brave man," I said. "You're not hot in that hoodie?" Nothing. Not a word.

"So, you just graduated high school, right?" He put his hands in his hoodie pouch and nodded.

"Well, congrats, man. Any ideas on college?"

"No," he said. His voice is low, and almost gentle, which kind of surprised me. I'm not sure what I was expecting. He didn't lash out or anything. Just said "no" and we kept walking. The lake glittered like a mirage under the morning sun.

"That's all right. I mean, you don't have to do college."

I sounded like the kid's estranged grandfather or something trying to figure out how to relate to the youth. At least, that's how I felt. I was trying to remember how I experienced the world when I was his age. 17 or whatever it was. As we neared the concrete wall at the waterfront, I was thinking how there was a period in high school when I got really quiet, started spending a lot of time in my room, and being on the internet way more than I needed to be. It's kind of crazy how primary the fake world can become. It can feel real, anyway. And it's so easy to curate. Just a few taps of your fingers and you have this profile, this image of who you think you're supposed to be; you can watch the most beautiful women in the world undress, and you can play sad white boy music on repeat. No one is stopping you from doing this. Presumably Jordan was doing all those things, plus loads of weed.

"Do you have any interests?" I said lamely.

He shrugged. "Not really," he said. Then, after a decisive pause: "I used to skateboard."

"Used to?"

"Yeah."

By then we'd reached the waterfront. I opened up the paint bucket and started mixing it up with a nearby stick. Jordan sat on the edge of the wall and bounced his shoes off its side.

"This shouldn't take too long," I said, handing him a paint roller. "Me and Zach did it last year in like an hour and a half."

"This got painted a year ago?"

"Tell me about it."

I started painting on one end, close to this grove of trees, with Jordan on the other. That wall is so pocked with holes that you have to take goops of paint to fill them in, so it all starts to slide and make lines. Jordan wasn't putting enough paint on the roller and had to press it hard to the wall to get anything on it. "Lather it on, man," I told him.

About twenty minutes passed when he pulled out his phone and started playing a screamo band I'd never heard of. I don't judge a guy for loving screamo, but it's not really my cup of tea, and the closer we got to each other, the irritation grew, grating against my internal need to be the glowing image of patience and kindness towards him. I'll play music fairly loud when I'm alone in the car, but when I'm with someone else, I get kind of self-conscious and usually don't play anything. I don't know why it's that way. But with other people it just seems like they have zero self-awareness. Plus, Jordan isn't supposed to have his phone. Jenni encourages people to pretty much abandon phones for the whole summer. "Tell your folks that you're going AWOL," she always says. "You don't need them here."

We were about ten feet away when I finally summoned the courage and said, "Hey man, I don't mind the music, but you know you're not supposed to have your phone at camp. You were supposed to turn it in at the beginning of orientation."

He looked at me, squinting through the sun and blinking against the heat index. It was like he didn't understand what I said. "It's not a huge deal," I told him. "It's just…you know. We all have to do it. Jenni takes it pretty seriously." I don't remember what else I said. Maybe rambled on about how it's important to have a focused mindset, to be fully invested in what you're doing and where you're at. All I remember is his distinctly taking the phone out of his pocket, turning down the music with his head bowed and lips pursed, and putting it back in his pocket as if this was a legitimate compromise. We finished painting. He hadn't done a very good job. It was still streaky and uneven. Thick lines of green paint rain into the grass, and with the first rain, would bleed into the water. We hardly talked at all on the way up to the cafeteria for lunch. It was a weird feeling, having zero influence on someone who you apparently have some authority over, or responsibility *for*—but I didn't know if I cared enough to push a seemingly small issue, and also wondered if my motivations would be mixed if I did. Did I really want him to have a distraction free summer, or did I just want to keep from being humiliated and have him do what I told him? I remember this kid who worked at camp a couple years ago who went ballistic when a camper didn't clean his plate off the right way in the cafeteria. He went on that night at Bible study about how this "new generation" had no respect for authority. I don't know.

One thing did sort of catch my interest on our walk back, though. Jordan was staring at the group of canoes by the lake, beyond the waterfront pond. He had turned the music off and knitted his brows.

"You ever canoe?" I asked him.

"Once," he said. Then a few seconds later he added, "A really long time ago."

Maybe that's how I'll get to him. Take him for a canoe ride or something.

Time for breakfast. Gotta go.

May 28th

Last night, Jordan left the cafeteria around the same time as Gabby and Reagan. It's their third summer working together, and they've formed a pretty strong pact. We tend to call them the "inseparables." But I noticed that they wanted nothing to do with Jordan, who walked a bit behind them with his hands in his pockets. He looked in their direction, and both girls are definitely attractive, and you could tell that he was struck by that and maybe even wanted to talk to them. But they just glanced at him behind their shoulders, grimaced at each other, and picked up the pace until they got back to the dorms.

I would have walked with him myself, but I had to help Zach move a shipment of coke boxes into the snack shack from a delivery truck. I probably should have asked Jordan to lend a hand, too, but he started walking down the loop towards the edge of camp, maybe to see the sunset or something.

"T-minus two days," said Zach.

"For what?"

"For Jordan to leave."

"Ah."

Jenni came in with a clipboard and went down a list, making sure we'd gotten everything we ordered. We stacked the last of the boxes in the corner of the room beneath the caterpillar band of duct and the humming freezers when Zach wiped his brow and asked, "Jenni, why'd you hire that kid?"

"Which kid?"

"Haha. You know who I'm talking about."

"You sound kinda cynical."

"No, I'm just curious. Nobody knows him and he just doesn't seem like the type who would want to work here."

Jenni wiped down the table in the kitchen with a wet rag and tossed it into a bucket, eyes invisible beneath her ballcap, then she sighed and crossed her arms, facing us. "I'm not sure," she said. "To be honest with you. The principal at Adler High School called me up and told me his situation, which is, to put it lightly, an absolute dumpster fire. His dad's long gone and his mom is addicted to oxycontin, and she's about to lose custody of him. That was probably too much information, but all that to say that basically he's on the verge of being homeless. Apparently he has a rich grandpa some-where in the area but he isn't really in the picture."

"Oh."

"Yeah. I just felt kind of called to let him work here. And it's hard, be-cause I know he's different, and I know he hasn't been obeying all the rules, like giving up his phone. I just feel like maybe we have to accept that he's not going to contribute all that much to camp. Camp might have to contribute more for *him*." Zach quietly nodded, ashamed, probably, of how coarsely he'd framed his question.

"I don't know what we're called to do—if we're supposed to evangelize to him or just let him be and hope that he can feel like he belongs here," Jenni added. She shrugged again and snatched a broom to sweep up some pizza crumbs by the grease vats.

"Yeah. I wasn't trying to question you about it. I was just wondering," said Zach. He glanced at me, eyes a little wider than usual, and went on, "Sometimes I just wonder if people like him would like it here or feel like a fish out of water. Like, is he even a Christian?"

"He said he was on his application form," said Jenni. "Although the details of his conversion story were sort of sparse. Apparently he accepted Jesus at Vacation Bible School when he was six years old. But I don't know. After hearing what he was going through I just felt like I couldn't *not* take him in."

"Yeah, no, that makes sense, makes sense."

Jenni didn't sound defensive, but there was just a speck in her tone that suggested she was trying to get some support for hiring Jordan. Zach wasn't the only one wondering what Jordan was doing here. I was starting to hear as much across the table in the cafeteria and in the common room. When Jordan slipped into morning meetings after breakfast he chose his own table by the window in the Snack Shack (after Zach and the twins and I had already sat down closer to the counter to hear Jenni talk) and stayed put there the whole time, quietly knocking his knuckles on the table. It wouldn't get *quiet* when he entered a room, per se, but the atmosphere shifted, and you could notice it, and staff members who might have felt comfortable blurting out whatever stories they had at hand would keep it to themselves. It's like spending three straight years with the same pair of roommates and then senior year the college makes all of you live with the Uzbekistani foreign exchange student, who, although he doesn't say a word to you, keeps you, just by his mere presence huddled over his laptop in the corner, from flailing around the apartment in your undies after class for no other reason except that you feel free enough to do it. In that situation, you have a couple options. Ring the Uzbekistani into the madness of your friend group and take the chances of scarring him for life, or quietly leave him alone to his own universe, which he probably prefers anyway, and do your best to host your insider shenanigans elsewhere.

That's the best I can describe it. And right now, I think everyone is opting for choice #2.

May 29th

The first camp is come and gone, and we've got a day off before the next one comes tomorrow. Writing this at an old desk in the attic above the boy's dorm. You have to lower a trapdoor staircase to get to it. There's not much else up here except a green bean bag with a human shaped imprint in its center and stuffing emerging from its seams. It's hot in the attic, but I set up a box fan in the window, which is pretty much cut straight into the plywood. It's like I'm one of those expatriate writers in Paris. A Hemingway or Fitzgerald scribbling away at the next great American novel. Would you agree, Professor Snodgrass?

I had late night duty refilling the water jugs in the recreation field last night. I was buzzing around in Jenni's Kawasaki mule vehicle and had the local pellet gun pistol on my hip; ever since Jerry got bitten by a coyote last year in the rec field, Jenni makes whoever is on water-filling duty take the pistol with them just in case the worst happens.

But I had this moment when I had stopped the engine, finished filling the last water jug, and looked up at the sky from beneath the canopy. The flame from the oil refinery blotted out some of the stars on the horizon, but the majority of the constellations remained brightly stippled. It occurred to me, sort of out the blue, that if God really existed—this eternal Being who indwells the everlasting present moment—then He *made* all that, every single iota and whale and cell, and that by extension He was looking at *me*, a very small part of that bigness who was nonetheless somehow vital to the health of the whole system. It felt like I was both at the center and periphery of existence at the same time. Charged with significance and dust, kingship and nothingness. It was awesome.

In the end, I don't think this feeling was very far off from terror. But that idea of the God Personage actually *looking* at me, and with a smile on His face at that—man, it was almost too much to handle. After what must have been thirty minutes of revery, I zipped back to the dorms high as a kite, like John the Baptist or something, ready to enlighten the world of the impending glory. For the time being, it seemed obvious that nothing in this world can ever really go all that wrong or go so wrong that it can't be corrected. I almost ran into the dorm room, breathing hard, but no one was there. So, I went into the common area and sat on the couch, catching my breath, squinting at the unfriendly phosphorescent lights, which

19

threatened to lull me back into artificiality. Lorrie came out from the girl's dorm. Her best friend, Carli, followed her, but then said she was going to the Snack Shack for some ice cream, and walked by me with a smile and a cocked eye indicating that I should behave myself in her absence.

Lorrie sat on the couch across from me. She really is so dang cute when she's in a pony tail and wearing no makeup. Like she's about to fall asleep on the couch on a lazy Sunday afternoon, a record player droning with Bob Dylan in the background. She asked me if I was all right and if I'd been playing basketball with the twins.

"No, I was filling the water jug in the rec field, near Jenni's house."

"You're breathing so hard."

"I just had…a moment."

She leaned forward with her elbows on her knees, those sharp caramel eyes blinking with ambiguity. "You're weird, and I'll never understand you." Then she sat back into the cushions.

"I'm telling you, Lorrie, I just had a moment in the field. It was amazing."

"Did you bring pot to camp, Hunter Saint?"

"What? No! Of course not."

She smiled, crossing her arms and popping gum. "I'm kidding. I could never see you doing that. That kid *Jordan*, however." We chuckled. "So, what, you…had a breakthrough or something?"

"Something like that." I told her I filled the last water jug, and happened to look up at the stars, and had this thought that if what we believe about God is real, that we should all be very terrified and happy. That was all.

"Wow," said Lorrie. She narrowed her eyes contemplatively, suggesting my experience had the powers of transference, and added, "That's really cool, Hunter. I'm happy for you."

"Sorry. I must sound kind of nuts. It's been hard to read the Bible lately, though. Camp Woodward is busy enough, so it's just hard. And I have to get this writing assignment done this summer—"

She crossed her legs, scratched an arm, tilted her head toward the ground.

It's so hard these days to be quiet with someone else. Especially when it's someone you have a lot of unspoken feelings and thoughts about. It's like silence is never silence when Lorrie and I are in the room alone together. No, it's the furthest thing from silence.

"Well," she said. "I'm glad you had that moment tonight. God is good. I wish that would happen to *me*."

"Yeah," I said. "Thanks. And…I'm sure it will. Go out to the rec field at night. You'll see." But by then, the original glory had somewhat ebbed away and given into a fraught scramble for repossession, and Jordan slinked into the common area and into the dorm room behind us. Lorrie added, "I still haven't talked to him."

"Yeah. Me neither, really."

So now I'm here in the attic not really sure what to do with the rest of my day. I picked up a historical novel about pioneers in the Appalachians but only read a few feet of it. It's about a young married couple trying to survive in the woods by themselves. They manage to build a cabin eventually, but then there's the trouble with getting clean water, ploughing new ground, and making sure they can defend themselves against all the beasts in the woods.

I am still thinking a lot about last night in the rec field. I read in Acts this morning: *Your young men will prophesy…*

Camp Woodward is a special place. You can always count on somebody having a transportive encounter with the Divine. Last night, though—that was a first for me.

It's making me think a little bit about my upbringing, my faith, and why experiences like that seem to be so few and far between. That seems fitting to include in a writing assignment like this, anyway. Like most of my friends, I was basically born in the church, raised in Sunday school, and swam in culturally Christian rivers all the way through high school. I accepted Jesus as my Lord and Savior when I was twelve years old at Crater's Creek, the biggest church camp west of the Mississippi River, Camp Woodward's gargantuan black hole of a competitor. I was trying to remember the day I got saved. It's kind of a blur. I remember a big, dark auditorium filled with thousands of other kids my age, a man waving his arms on the stage, an altar call, and then a flood of repentant souls coursing down the aisles. Had I made any kind of "decision" that night? I don't know. All I can recall is that I walked down the aisle along with a dozen or so other kids from our church, someone gave me a flyer with bullet points on it, and I got added to a tally sheet. Every morning, they rang the bell for every soul that got saved the night before.

I do remember one thing about my conversion. I remember thinking that I should never have any problems ever again. The speaker said that Jesus is the answer for everything, that he changes everything, and I intended on holding him to it. Jesus really does change everything, after all, just maybe not everything at once. I thought I'd never do a bad thing, have a bad thought, dislike anybody, or have any kind of remaining sinful blemish in me ever again. They said Jesus checked us into heaven at the moment of salvation, and that was enough to send me beaming on the bus ride home, a new man at twelve years old.

Maybe that's why I got so down and out the second I got home, and Carey took too long in the bathroom, and Dad told me to shovel dog crap in the backyard, and Mom reminded me that seventh grade was three weeks away, and like the drop of a hat, the past week at Crater's Creek acquired a film of mildew and my brand-new, born-again heart seemed right back where it was eight days before. Impatient, undisciplined, and morose at the thought of another schoolyear. Now, post-salvation, being angry didn't just mean being angry. It meant total betrayal of who I was. *Christians don't get angry! What's all this about negative emotions and feeling sorry for myself??* Even worse, it might mean I was never saved to begin with. If I struggle with *that* particular sin, does that mean I have to go down to the altar all over again? How can I ever know if it's for real? What about those tears shed at the passing of my cat, Ginger, and the apparent angel on my shoulder, whispering, *C'mon, stop being a baby. Would Jesus cry over some stupid dead cat?*

Fast forward ten years, after listening in on hundreds of sermons from Pastor Bill who also seemed to think that the altar call meant an instant cure of the human condition, and seeing a pre-salvation, manically depressed, heavy-death-metal-garbed Jordan sparked the old anxiety. If I don't love this kid, then I'm probably not a real Christian. That's the syllogism of my life.

Maybe I need to go out to the water jug in the rec field more often.

June 1st

Today's camp is rolling in in a couple of hours.

Last camp, I was in the Snack Shack for most afternoons, but today it's on to the lifeguarding. The real stuff of my job description. Which means today is Jordan's first day as a lifeguard, too. It's remarkable to me that he passed the swim tests, but he did, and got certified with CPR, and seemed to do all these things as obediently as one could. I have no idea what he did on the day off. I never saw him around camp, even though I walked around the loop a couple of times and went for a swim last night around six. In any case, he's doing all right so far as I can tell. Jenni pats him on the back when she passes him, and he sweeps up the peas and crumbs after dinner and gives kids their Dr. Peppers and Gatorades when they ask for it in the Snack Shack. He just doesn't talk, and he doesn't give up his phone.

In Jenni's office. She's twisting her hair and studying her computer monitor. An email is studying her back. Her walkie-talkie is setting on the desk atop some unruly papers and manila folders, beeping with a little red light at the top. I asked how she was doing and she said that this camp had goofed their original numbers and was bringing not 200 kiddos but *800* kiddos, and would like to have late nights at the Snack Shack from 8-11 p.m. thank you very much. And all these from modest Miami, Oklahoma. "LORD," she said, slapping her desk with both hands lifting her chin to the ceiling. "800 is capacity. We have 12 people on staff."

"Volunteer the peasants," I said. "Scour the countryside, pluck up all panhandlers and listless high school kids."

"At this point, maybe."

She clacked away at the monitor and spun in her chair to face me. We talked a little bit about yesterday. After a while I told her she hadn't really answered my question about how she was doing. Not really. She scratched her head and then Joyce the associate director walked in, holding a bundle of T-shirts and going, "Whew! They finally came in."

All for now.

Zach and I took Jenni's mule down some old trails last night, way later than we should have. He drove and I shone the flashlight into the woods looking for...what? I don't know why we go on these escapades, but we do it every year. We do see some cool stuff, honestly. Last year we spotted a bobcat hunched on a dead oak branch. Last night a herd of deer skittered across the trail, snorting, the couple of bucks jouncing their racks, looking tough. But maybe we just do it for the kicks. It's a loud engine and we're dudes. We like the way the mule romps and bangs and never breaks, no matter how steep the creek or gnarly the roots and rocks. We went all the way to the edge of the lake and then alongside the dam, down a ways until we reached the heavy-leaning barn, which is probably going to fall this summer if Jerry and Gabe don't rip it down first. Jenni told Zach to please not flip the dang thing or topple down the hill on the other side of the dam, which is a considerable distance and bungled with ant hills. He asked her what she was so worried about, and she said she was worried about us. And also a liability suit.

Coyotes yipped nearby. There are never as many, though, as you might think. It's like the second the sun goes down, God lights an invisible fire under the butt of every coyote in the world, and they just go crazy.

We stopped on the dam on the way back, but once the engine stopped, I leaned back and found the same spread of stars flaking the sky, and the quiet water, and the rim of trees that chattered with locusts and whippoorwills and tree frogs. I wanted to tell Zach about the other night. When I looked up with the empty water jug and had that flash of insane wonder, and how I was equally confused how that sense seemed to leave me so quickly—how explaining it to Lorrie was like trying to talk to a stone. And that's not because of Lorrie. It's just to say that I don't know why words always go butchered down into nothing when it comes time to relay something important to somebody. Why nothing I say is ever what I really mean or fails to correspond to the thoughts and feelings behind the words. Of course, I didn't know how to say any of this to Zach. He started whistling to himself. He took his hat off and brushed his mullet backwards, then started singing a sad Toby Keith song to himself. So, I didn't even try to talk to him about God. It's just so weird how little we talk about it, about Christ, about all that stuff, right smack dab in a Christian camp. We talk about it in Bible studies, yeah, but it's cramped, filled with convictions no one actually has. The real pains and sins go unsaid.

Instead of trying to talk to Zach about transcendence, I sighed and said, "You talk to Jordan at all yet?"

"No," Zach said. "I haven't really, to tell you the truth. Like, I want to, and Jenni asked me about it, same as she did for you."

"So? I haven't talked to him much either, really. He doesn't seem to be doing so bad."

"I don't know, man. It just feels like we've got nothing in common, or that he doesn't want to talk to me at all. It's sort of tough to approach a person like that."

"Yeah. No, you're right." I told him about painting the wall near the waterfront. How he still had his phone, and when I told him that it wasn't allowed, all he did was turn the music down and say nothing in response. "He seemed interested in the canoes," I said.

"The canoes?"

"Yeah. He stared at the canoes on our way back to the cafeteria. I think he even looked behind his shoulder once we'd passed 'em."

"Hmm. All right."

"So maybe we could take him for a canoe ride. I don't know. Who's to know?" This too is a dimension of life that was a doozy to articulate. This weird sense of responsibility for the soul of this human being. He probably doesn't know Jesus. That's just guessing. Usually, you have to love Jesus to work at Camp Woodward, but Jenni is known to make the occasional exception. "Sometimes you need camp more than camp needs you," she always tells us in orientation. I've found this to be true. And I don't mean money. Maybe that's what Christ meant when He said giving is better than receiving, because really giving is receiving in its truest, though subtlest, form. And that's not self-congrats for being an overly grateful guy.

"I'll take him out, sure. You bet," said Zach. "If he wants to, I'll take him. Heck, bring Lorrie along, and we'll all go. The veterans take the rookie out for a boat ride."

It sounded virtuous. Tremors of thunder sounded somewhere off east, far away. "It might rain tomorrow," I said.

"On our day off."

"Yeah."

"Another day off already."

"Don't think we've ever had a camp close up shop this early."

"I'm all right with it."

We continued with that kind of talk for another five minutes. Talk that really is talk about nothing. And I don't say that in a bitter way. But come on. That's really all most of this talking stuff is.

Later that night, I had just turned off my lamp and was heading to bed when I heard someone get up and open the dorm room door. It wasn't Zach. He was already snoring. And the twins were still playing basketball on the outdoor courts. After a minute I slipped out of bed and went into the common room and peeked out the window. Jordan ambled down the stone road with his hands in his pockets, scrawny elbows bouncing against his sides. His hair covered his bowed head but he didn't have his phone with him, and from all appearances he was heading to the waterfront. Should I have followed him? I went downstairs and stepped on the concrete walk, kicking away the June bugs and dead crickets. I even stepped into the gravel and took a breath to call his name. But I didn't. He took out a cigarette, or a joint of weed, one of the two, and lit it just as he escaped the glare of the floodlight from atop the rec barn.

How are you supposed to follow someone like that into *darkness* like that? I tried praying about it. God give me the courage to enter into that darkness. Is he going off to the canoes? I ended up justifying my avoidance by deciding that he wanted to be left alone. If a person insists on being left alone, can you be friends with them? I just wasn't so sure I've even tried is the problem. What do you want me to do, God? I mean, I've got all of two more months to reach out to the kid, right?

Lorrie just walked into the cafeteria holding her bible and C.S. Lewis. She got coffee at the bar and is mixing it with sugar. Why is everything she does suddenly so glorious?

June 3rd

The big camp is here. 800 kids, not including sponsors and pastors, as promised.

Last night we did the tractor rides through the woods and I was delegated to be the ghost story teller. I used to hate it. I never had any good stories, and I have a low voice so it's hard for anybody to hear me over the tractor engine. Then a couple years ago, Johnny, who used to work at the waterfront here, told me to the tall tale of old man Kyle. Kyle was an old homeless man who had apparently shacked up in the woods and was known to haunt the outskirts of camp from time to time. You can't quite discern his hoot owl call from a real hoot owl. You have to listen real close and try to hear any human breathing to tell if it's really him. Of course, Johnny would ask somebody to dress up like old man Kyle and hang out by the tractor trail in the woods. Once, Zach pretended to be Kyle, and he climbed up in a tree overhanging the trail and crouched there in the darkness like a vulture prowling for corpses, and when the tractor came bumbling along with the kids on the trailer, he fell out of the tree on accident and broke his wrist. He also almost got ran over. A few kids fainted because they thought it was really old man Kyle and that moreover the geezer had decided to die right in front of them. Zach missed some of football because of the injury. He was sore about it for a year.

Whether Kyle is real or not remains a mystery. He's not real. Duh. Or is he? Up to the kids to decide. Although once Jenni told me that, years ago, an old man in overalls and a long beard with a walking stick to boot came out of the woods one day and started telling kids about the end of the world. That they'd better repent. Even though they were children, they needed God more than anything and that in God's eyes this whole world was a child, and relative to the age of the universe we were all but larvae, unready for the sun. Jenni said the message wasn't too much different from the evening services, but still—it was crazy that this random guy had come out of the woodwork looking like an Old Testament prophet, speaking like one, jigging like one. Jenni said that Jerry confronted the prophet, and they exchanged some dialogue in tongues. To me that seems like further validation that the dude was Spirit-inspired, or at least convincingly off his rocker, but in the end, he walked back into the woods at gunpoint and no one saw him again.

So I talked about Kyle the Prophet on the hayride that night for about eight rides. It was about ten p.m. and Jerry was taking calls for a final ride, and about ten kids came aboard, and one of them was Jordan, who up until that point had been manning one of the inflatables and making sure kids weren't wrestling on them. He wasn't supposed to be there, but he came aboard and sat next to me at the helm without a word and brushed the hair out of his eyes and took a sip of a Mountain Dew. The inflatable jungle billowed in the party barn like an organism that's supposed to be extinct. "Oh, hey man," I said. "You made it."

He nodded and leaned back. A tiny girl holding a corndog with a glowstick looped around her neck asked if I was going to tell them a scary story, and I said maybe, and she said I'd better not tell anything *too* scary because then she couldn't sleep that night. I said no promises. The other kids talked and hooted and whispered, and Jordan still said nothing.

Jerry started driving the tractor toward the loop, which begins at the rim of the woods next to the worship sanctuary. It juts out briefly into the back rec field and then snakes back into the trees down an eroded road and then along the bank of the lake for about a quarter of a mile. I started telling my ghost story just before we got to the rec field. Everyone went quiet. They huddled with their hands clasped, popsicle-stained faces slanted up. I said, leaning forward, eyes wide, chewing a blade of straw,

"Y'all ever hear of old man Kyle?"

"No!" they whispered.

"Well you're about to. Just to set a ground rule—try to be *very* quiet or else he might hear you. Rumor has it he only comes close to camp when it's dark so he can look like a tree stump or something. So just whispering. Got it? Okay. So a few years ago, my buddy Johnny decided to go for a swim in the lake, the one right over there, only he decided this time to do it *at night*. If you haven't noticed, Camp Woodward has some of the best stars you'll ever see, and Johnny wanted to lay on his back in the water and take it all in out in the middle of the lake. So he did. He went out on an evening in early June and started swimming out to the middle. It was a perfect night for it. There wasn't a cloud in the sky and, and it was moonless, too. The locusts were going crazy like they are now and he was even having a moment with God out there—praying and thanking the Lord for creating such beauty in nature. And so he got to the middle of the lake, and started floating on his back like he planned, when he heard something. Something in the water. He straightened up so his head was still above the water, but saw, coming out of the darkness, a canoe. Only, there wasn't anybody rowing it. It was empty. And I should also mention that there wasn't any wind, either. It was a completely still night. So there was no logical way the canoe could have been floating along all by itself. It was coming right for him. He called out, 'Hello! Who's there?' But no one answered. So, Johnny swam back towards the dock a few yards, and turned around to watch the canoe pass on by from a distance. He wasn't sure, but it looked like the thing vanished into the night as it slipped by. Weird, right? That's not the worst of it, though. Johnny was pretty well spooked, like you might expect, so he decided to call it quits and swim back to the dock—the one we're about to drive by here in about two minutes. But when he started to swim home, he saw something else—this time it was the figure of a man standing on the dock, completely still, looking out at him, waiting for him. You guys have seen the lake. There's not many places to swim to. The dock is your best bet. But of course, Johnny wasn't about to crawl up by a stranger, especially after the incident with the canoe just happened. So he panicked, turned right, and started for the steep dam on the south side of the lake. As he tread water, he tried not to look to his left, but couldn't help it after long, and saw that the man on the dock was tracking him along the bank, right in step with him. Johnny turned back around. The mystery man turned around, too. Johnny went underwater and swam about twenty feet and then came up quiet and low, swimming beaver style towards the dock again. Still the man tracked him without even bothering to look up. The man was old and dressed in overalls and had a scary gleam in his eye.

"So before long, Johnny was out of breath. His heart was beating. His muscles were tense and he had a terrible cramp in his side. He couldn't stay out in the lake much longer without drowning. So, he said a prayer, gritted his teeth, and headed straight for the dock to meet his fate. He didn't look up. Not to the right or the left. He just swam straight ahead without a thought to what might happen to him. Finally, he grabbed the edge of the dock, gasping for breath, and hauled himself up, half expecting a knife to stab him in the back. But that didn't happen. He rolled over on his back, and the only thing he saw were those stars that he'd originally come out to see in the first place. He stood up and scanned the waterfront area. There was no one. He looked into the trees, into the shallows, and even checked underneath the canoes. But there was no old man.

"So to this day, neither Johnny or anybody else knows who that old man was exactly or where that crazy canoe came from. We just got to calling him 'Kyle,' named after a kid who used to work here but then disappeared mysteriously... But you don't have to worry. That was last summer and we haven't had any old man Kyle sightings yet this year. Oh, look, guys! We're coming up next to the dock!"

I had got this crowd good. They were shivering in their sweaty seats of hay, looking in dread at the dock bobbing lightly among the reeds in the moonlight. Jordan leaned over and said, "Did that really happen?"

"No," I whispered. "Course not." Jordan leaned away again, frowning.

"Remember, y'all, that was just a story—or was it? In any case, you're safe with me and Jerry. Jerry's got a good gun that he uses to shoot armadillos, but if some crazy guy ever charges into camp he can ward him off, too."

"Jerry's really got a pistol?" Jordan asked.

I laughed. "Yep. Keeps it in his nightstand."

"Is *that* supposed to be old man Kyle?" It was the girl again. She chewed her corndog stick and broke it with her fingers.

"What, who?"

"That weird lookin' guy sitting next to you!" It took me a hot second to realize she was talking about Jordan. Jordan said nothing.

"He looks scary!" said a fat lad in the back. "Is he supposed to be scary?"

"No!" I said. "No, this isn't old man Kyle. This is my friend, Jordan. He works here just like I do."

"Oh. I thought maybe it was part of the thing," said the girl. "Like, he would end up being the old man and then pretend to kill us all or something."

"Nope. Definitely not." These crazy kids.

By that time, we were churning up the sandy hill. We reached the cafeteria and then pulled up next to the Party Barn, and the kids all filed out, losing their terror. Jordan got up, too. "I'm sorry about that, man," I said. Jordan sniffed. I think it was supposed to be a laugh. "No worries," he said. "I am a pretty scary-looking dude."

He walked over to help put up the inflatable. And of course, when I met Lorrie and Zach to walk back to the dorms, we heard an owl hooting just a branch or two above our heads.

June 4th

A water line broke last night behind the maintenance shed. Jerry radioed us around ten p.m. and the guys all filed out there to see what was up. The water was bubbling up a through the clay in a hole around three feet deep, turning it into red brown soup. Zach and Jerry slid into the hole, mud up almost to their waist, and shoveled out the slop into a pile behind them. Their faces creased with effort. Teeth and biceps clenched. I don't know if there's any combined element heavier than mud plus water. The twins watched, and I shone a flashlight in the hole since it was already getting dark. No one knew where Jordan was. He hadn't been at the Snack Shack like he was supposed to.

"We gotta get this patched up tonight," said Jerry. He cursed under his breath. His face shone beet red beneath his flat bill cap. He spat tobacco into his work. "Gross," said Zach.

"Oh, don't be a baby."

"800 kids and sponsors here without running water," Rory said. "Yikes."

"Yeah, I know, *Rory*," said Jerry. I laughed to myself. Every summer something like this happens. Last year a tornado ripped through Stanley Station five miles south and left the entire county without electricity for two days. The camp had to jet out early while the staff lived in darkness. It does make you realize how dependent we are on this whole elaborate system of technology. Or I guess it's not always so elaborate. Just look at the pipeline. It's a plastic tube that runs through the ground.

"How are we going to fix it?" I said.

"I don't freaking know. Jenni won't answer her phone."

"Jenni knows how to fix water pipes?"

"No."

"So why call her?"

"Hunter, just shut up, okay?" He tossed slop at my feet.

"Need a break, Zach?"

He glanced up at me, panting, and wiped mud off his scruff. After a pause, he rejected the high road and said, "Yeah sure," and clambered up to solid ground. I rolled up my shorts to my mid thighs and got on in with the shovel in hand.

"We just gotta get the water out of here enough to expose the pipe, and then we can cut out the bad part and fuse a new piece into it."

"You know how to do that?"

"You ask a lot of questions."

"Gabe knows how to do it, then?"

Jerry sighed. "Yeah, Gabe knows how to do it."

"Where's Gabe?" asked Zach.

"I don't know."

"Shouldn't you know? I mean, who else is supposed to know?"

Jerry hurled his shovel heavenward and crawled out of the pit, growling so primally I had to check the woods for creatures.

"You pansies sit tight, and I'll go find Gabe," he said, swinging into his golf cart. He zoomed off with his head bent forward in mock concentration, leaving the rest of us in a darkening evening and suddenly responsible for the comfort and cleanliness of 800 kiddos. Zach said, "Welp," and then slipped back into the muck next to me. The twins illuminated the mess with their flashlights and also raked the piles of mud into little mountains. I felt like the sludge never got much lower. I mean, we were using scooping liquid out with shovels for Pete's sake.

"Hey boys, get some buckets, will you?"

"Yeah, okay."

Minutes passed and Gabe and Jerry hadn't shown up.

"This is just our luck," said Zach, dipping his plastic chalice into the grime. "Girls are in the dorms, sleeping. Jenni's nowhere to be found. And hey what about Jordan? What's *he* up to?"

"Just keep scooping. I can see the stupid pipe."

The pipe showed itself every time I plunged my bucket into the goop. A gash the width of a finger oozed water.

"How'd this happen?" I said.

"Heck if I know. Apparently Gabe was using the backhoe out here to clear some brush. That's what Jerry said."

"Gabe's getting old."

The story didn't really make sense. I had a hunch that Jerry had struck the line himself, and that that explained his stingy mood and moreover why Gabe wasn't around at all, but nobody wanted to say it. Jerry is probably going to inherit this place someday, maintenance-wise, and he's always done a good job. One mishap shouldn't derail his aspirations. He's the handiest dude we know. We switched places with the twins around midnight, and I decided to walk over to Jenni's house just to see if she was around.

The gravel road from behind the maintenance shed led me by the line of dumpsters. An armadillo scurried across the road in front of me, blind and armored. It rooted around in the grass and then darted into the trees like a malignant robot. Cicadas were so loud it almost behooved me to cover my ears at one point. And there was another call of the hoot owl making lonely conversation with itself in some knot of an oak tree down the boulder-pocked hill. I wiped my mud banked hands on my shorts and crossed my arms. The white line of the road unspooled in front of me like a familiar trail leading to what's yet unknown.

The porch light was on at Jenni's house. She sat in her rocking chair dressed in sweatpants and a tank-top, looking out over the back rec field.

"Hey Hunter," she greeted me when I was halfway across the yard.

"Hey," I said. "What's up?"

"Not a whole lot. Sorry about the water leak."

"We'll fix it. Did Jerry come by?"

"Yeah. I sent him to go get Gabe."

"Oh, okay. He hasn't shown up for a while."

I sat down in the other rocking chair and let out a breath. We rocked back and forth for a few seconds, and then Jenni said, "Jordan's leaving tomorrow."

I stopped rocking and leaned forward. "What? Really? Why?"

Jenni shrugged and picked at a fingernail. "He came by after dinner and said this wasn't it for him, and that his mom is coming to get him tomorrow afternoon. He said he'd work until then, though."

"Shoot."

I immediately thought of the dumb hayride and those kids asking me if he was old man Kyle. "That's all he said?" I asked.

"Pretty much. I tried to tell him that it gets better, and that the first two weeks are the hardest, and that kind of spiel, but I could tell he wasn't gonna go for it."

"Shoot," I repeated, and narrowed my brow. "Maybe I can talk to him."

"You can if you want. I always knew it was a longshot having some-one like that at camp. It happens every few years, and I think that hiring someone who's sort of different, or struggling, would really benefit them. Maybe it's arrogant to think that. It's just a church camp in the middle of the woods—it can't save anybody."

"You were being generous and kind," I said. Jenni kept teasing her fingernail. "It's who you are. A lot of people come through here not know-ing what to expect and then leave better off than before. For other kids, they just bow out, and there's nothing you can really do about that except let them do it and hope they stay in touch."

"Yeah. That's true."

"Well, I'm sorry, though."

"I'm sorry for him. He doesn't seem like a bad kid."

"Yeah."

We sat there in silence for a while. I knew I needed to go back to the boys but didn't want to just yet. Sometimes you can tell when a person is drawing from your presence in a way that's even better than words. I didn't have anything to say to Jenni that she didn't know already. Our wisdom scales will forever be skewed in her favor. But I could tell she felt bad. I felt bad too. But honestly, and I hate to write this down, but I felt a little bit relieved. There's just no denying that Jordan makes the other staffers uncomfortable. His sour, pale face, pickled with acne, his greasy locks of black hair brushing his shoulders, his teeth stained and rotted by years of Mountain Dew, his black, stinking shirts—God, what am I doing? Didn't you call us to *love* people like that? Because in a way, you know, that's all of us? So what if he doesn't have great hygiene or that his favorite movie is probably *Saw*? Is it a Christian thing to overlook all that stuff and attribute whatever deficiencies you see in a person to context and a painful background? Supposing he really is a psychopath? I don't know. I don't know. Sometimes people rub you the wrong way. It's human. But I hate that it happens to me, too. I feel like it shouldn't happen to me. I'm supposed to like everybody. There's not supposed to be a mean or exclusionary bone in my body. What would Jesus do? Do we ever actually ask ourselves that?

I got up to go after Jenni brought me a coke from inside, but before I could step off the porch, Jerry zoomed along in his golf cart leaving angry puffs of dust in his wake. He strode across the lawn.

"Can't find my gun," he said to Jenni. "Do you know where it is?"

"What gun?"

"My *pistol*, I cain't *find* it!"

"All right, settle down. Why do you need it?"

"Because I was going to shoot a couple of armadillos after we fixed the pipe. I saw about five just on my way over here."

"Well, I don't have it," said Jenni.

"*Somebody* has it!" He turned to me. "Do you know anything about it?"

I shook my head. "No man, I'm sorry. Maybe you left it somewhere and forgot about it?"

"Nah, no way. I remember it was in my nightstand this morning because I always check just to make sure it's still there. My grandpa left me that gun."

"I'm sure it's around somewhere, Jerry."

Jerry sat down on the concrete porch and took off his hat and spat into the grass and then beat his fist as hard as he could on the ground with his teeth clenched and that same primal growl braiding up through his throat until it became a full-blown scream. Jenni stood up and we exchanged glances.

"Jerry, if you're going to freak out, do it somewhere else, please."

Jerry bowed his head and wheezed something indiscernible. Jenni went up to him and put her hand on his shoulder. I stood back a ways chewing my lip, hands sweating through the mud. Jerry shook his head, wiped his eyes, and then got up and walked back to his golf cart. He drove away slowly and left a big silence behind him.

I walked back over to the hole. Gabe was there in the mud, muttering to himself. He had a device that held the new section of pipe in place and fused it with the rest of the pipe, and after this was done, he told Jerry to turn the water back on. Once Jerry did, we all hustled back to the dorms and tested the faucets and showers. My faucet gurgled red water at first, spat air and a slightly clearer stream for thirty seconds, and then turned into its usual calcium rich yield after that.

"We did it boys!" Zach shouted. Jordan came into the dorms and passed Jerry on his way.

"Yeah we did!" laughed Rory, smacking James on the back. "That's how it's done!" I didn't remind everyone that the most we'd done was scoop mud slop from a hole and that the real heroism belonged to Gabe.

I turned the water off and sidled up to Jordan's bed. He was stuffing clothes into his backpack. "Hey man," I said. He turned around, red-eyed and expressionless. "I'm sorry you're heading out."

It was the only time I ever saw him smile, and this smile was slight, of course, but it wasn't fake. "Yeah," he said. "Me too."

When we turned the lights off and Zach drifted off to sleep on the other side of the nook, I put my hand on my heart and just felt it beat for a while. Sometimes I do that when I can't see my own hand in front of me, it's so dark.

June 5th

I don't really know where to start. How to start. It's night now in Jenni's office and there are still cop cars in the lot. God. God. God. I don't think I can write about this just now. My hand's shaking. Why won't it stop shaking? Mom and Dad both called seven times apiece and I answered and said, yes, I was all right, everyone was all right, thank Christ.

He, Jordan, he stood in the middle of the field, near the main water jug where I'd had my transcendent experience, the field full of kids, pulled out Jerry's pistol and shot it into the air five times in a row. Pop pop pop pop pop. It's still popping in my head now. Then he settled the barrel beneath his chin and screamed.

Zach, Lorrie, and I heard the shots, saw the kids duck and flee like mice escaping a rainstorm. Jordan, though, didn't shoot the sixth shot. He chucked the gun at the ground. It went off when it landed. The bullet pinged off the post of the volleyball set or maybe the wall of the party barn. He then ran in circles a couple of times, darting left, then right, until finally deciding to sprint towards the waterfront with his head set wildly back and his eyes rolling like some demonic mustang. Lorrie screamed, hanging on my arm. Zach stammered and tensed, raising his fists and skittering backwards. I just stood there openmouthed as Jordan got closer, closer, letting out this terrible wail that I still hear as I'm writing these words. "Get him!" Zach screamed. "Lorrie, get off him, c'mon!" Old man Kyle was right. It really did feel like the end of the world during that two-minute span of time.

The next five minutes were nuts. I told Lorrie to get inside the Snack Shack and stay there until I came for her. She did, as Carli and Gabby and James and Rory converged from the dorms, shielding their eyes against the sun. Jenni flew out of the office, radioing everybody and dialing the police at the same time. "Get inside, now, get inside, anywhere inside!" she shouted over and over again. The kids, all 800 of them, huddled in the rec barn with their pale-faced youth ministers shepherding them in hordes, while Zach and I saw Jordan zoom down the sand hill not twelve yards away from us. "Let's go!" Zach shouted. We started after him, challenged to make up about twenty yards of distance, and Jenni screamed at us to stop. We didn't stop.

Whatever tricks Jordan had hidden up his sleeve, one of them was definitely his crazy fast running abilities. He was at the water before we even reached the shallow end of the waterfront. And Zach was a running back in college. Jordan shoved a canoe out into the shoals by the dock and thrashed at the water with the paddle. He veered sharply but straightened out once he picked up some speed, heading for the channel where the lake narrows and bleeds off into a hundred little creeks leading into a hundred different spots in the woods.

Zach picked a canoe off the rack and hurled it right-side up on the grass. "Paddles!" he screamed. "Where are they?" Usually, they're strapped to the belly of the boat, but they were gone, and what's more, the canoe was shanked full of holes. He must have gone down on the off day and stabbed them with a fence post, or something such. "Son of a bitch!" Zach screamed. "Hey! Get back here! Get back here!" Zach stumbled into the shallows like he was going to swim, waving his arms. The reeds were parted where Jordan had launched the canoe, but the kid had already rounded the corner of the channel peninsula, leaving nothing but a bobbing wake of water behind him.

He skittered off quick as a water bug and that was that.

The quiet was heavy and sick after he was gone, with Zach gasping for breath in the water and me on my hands and knees in the grass, holding my chest, about to retch. We didn't know if he had hurt anybody at that point or not. It looked like he just shot in the air and ran. By the time we'd started back up the sand hill, speechless, a helicopter stammered off in the distance, and a line of police cars charged down the dirt road to Camp Woodward.

I wrote the events. There. It's done. What else do you want from me, right now, conscience?

Jerry walked into Jenni's office about a half hour later, sweating and trying to catch his breath.

"They found my gun!" he said. "Laying out in the middle of the rec field. What did I tell you? I told you that kid was up to no good."

"Easy," I said. "Nobody could have known."

"How did he *find* it?" Jerry bellowed.

"I don't know."

"Somebody must've told him where I'd hidden it. There was nothing messed up in the house at all. He didn't look *anywhere* else."

Jenni was clutching her head and I was rolling my forehead on the heel of my palm and just then remembering that yes, somebody must've indeed told him where the stupid gun was and that it was stupid someone was me: I had done it on the hayride two nights ago. He asked me about Jerry's gun and I told him without thinking twice, as if this would be a conversation starter. Jerry stomped out of the room before I could even think about telling him.

"Jesus," I whispered.

Jenni is now at her office desk, a couple hours after shots were fired, writing something down on a sticky note. She's just gotten off the phone about three hundred mothers, around half of who are demanding she tender her resignation, effective immediately, and that Camp Woodward shut its gates forever. After every phone call her wrist starts to shake a little bit more and her face gets a little paler.

She says the cops will keep looking for him, but nothing yet. Just a couple hours and this great camp of 800 kids has gone home, leaving our little society almost empty, maybe for good. Jenni's laying her head down on her desk. There's a black, leather-bound journal next to her. When she raised her head, I asked what the book was.

"His journal."

June 6th

There's so much still unknown and I feel like my brain's been about to bust at the seams over the last few hours, but I'll do my best.

The cops have left camp but they're still making rounds within a twenty-mile radius and are sending teams with dogs into the woods. Lorrie leaned on my shoulder for an hour after dinner by the dock. She came up while I was sitting there staring at the lake, running the events through my head over and over. I told her I was going to look for him. Tonight. She said please, please don't. Not even the state troopers can find him, so that means you *definitely* can't find him.

"He wasn't going to kill anyone," I said.

"How do you know?"

"He was scared." I was recalling that ashen, wailing face, flying past me like a white moon. Maybe he had it all planned out. Fire every round into the crowd of children and then off to the canoes, off to drown himself in one of the hidden channels. He waited until the kids were all on the rec field, waited, maybe, for me, Lorrie, and Zach to weave into view, and then he fired the shots like he was striking some flare in the darkness.

"I'm going to look for him," I told her. "There's one canoe that's all right. He didn't ruin them all. Do you see?"

"Hunter."

"Look." I went over to the canoe rack and ran my hands up and down the one on the bottom rung. He had mottled the others and left one untouched, absolutely untouched. "He wanted someone to come after him."

"It was an accident," Lorrie said. "That doesn't mean anything."

"How do you know?"

"He was scared. He didn't know what he was doing." Lorrie stood up and put her face into her hands. "He ran right past you, Hunter. He could've killed some of those kids."

"Hey, hey."

She sobbed and wrapped her arms around me and pressed her ear to my chest and we were just like that for a few minutes next to all these useless canoes with the bottom one suspiciously intact, ready to sail. You know, I've never actually canoed down the narrow channel of Lake Woodward. We usually just swim the lake and leave the canoes alone. I made up my mind, though—I had to look for this kid that Jenni told me to look after.

Maybe because it was my fault, and I knew it was my fault. But it was like God himself was telling me to do it.

"Don't do it," Lorrie said.

June 7th

You don't think you're afraid of the dark until you canoe into a lake channel at midnight. The stars and waning gibbous moon didn't help me. I brought my high-powered flashlight with me, sitting in the back of the boat, quietly rowing as Camp Woodward slept unsoundly behind.

The next two camps are canceled by mutual agreement, and the calls for Jenni's resignation have fortunately been somewhat tempered by the other dimensions of the story. But so far, the end of June and all of July are still intact, and no staffer has jumped ship yet. Surprisingly, no parent has swooped to rescue their baby from imminent harm. That's really something when you think about it. The cops think Jordan might have died somewhere on the run, and that it is only a matter of time before they turn up with the body in the Green River, or some cow pond on a rancher's land, or maybe in this narrow strait.

But this canoe. It would have been the easiest boat in the bunch to poke. It would have been the first one he'd seen, but it was completely fine—not a scratch on it. And only one other canoe.

Zach's been really quiet since it happened. Today he was folding his clothes by his bed while I just laid there, staring at the wire bedframe above me. The twins were on the phone a lot with their grandma, who they live with, but managed to convince her that they were okay, that they needed to stay at camp. Never mind that there was a psychopath running around the woods plotting his next attack, Grandma said over speaker phone. Zach looked up when he heard that, straight faced and silent. He was a crazy son of a you-know-what, she went on, nihilistic atheist...a radical liberal, by all accounts, in collusion with the Satanists, an affront to this Christian nation. The twins took her off speaker and hung up about a minute later, and laid on their backs in their bunks without saying anything.

As the hours went on, though, I couldn't help but be grateful. It could have been ten times worse. It *has* been ten times worse. But everyone is still pretty shook. The girls keep crying together in twos and threes in the common room. A few of them went home for a week to recuperate, but no one really wants to leave camp. No one here really has any other place to go except to their dark rooms and cell phones.

After the lights went out, I felt wide awake, even though the last few nights, no one in the dorms has gotten more than a few hours of sleep. Jerry and Gabe have been making rounds in their mules at night, locking doors and perching on top of the hill near the camp entrance with binoculars and .22 rifles. Of course, they haven't seen anything. Only armadillos and possums and one timber rattlesnake, a five-footer that Jerry killed with a crowbar and is skinning to put up on his wall in his trailer house. But they're not going to find him. And what would they do with him if they did find him? Take him to the police, sure, but for what crime? He didn't try to kill anybody. He just scared the living crap out of us and showed all of 800 plus people that he *could have* killed, but for some reason, chose to hold off and take those few moments of fixed attention instead.

Feeling distracted. Exhausted but wakeful. Supposed to be going home this afternoon, carpooling with Lorrie, while Zach is going home to Arkansas for the next few days. It's seven in the morning and I decided to go to the cafeteria to write again before the trip. Down the hill, the water is gray and still, and two does jounced from beyond a hedge and hightailed into the woods behind the rack of broken canoes.

I didn't get far last night. The flashlight, when I did use it, cut into sections of forest, revealing circles of heavy foliage and brown shallows. The light would calm my nerves a bit, or so I thought, but really it put a new kind of fear in me. At any moment, it seemed like the beam would land right on Jordan's pale face sticking up out of the reeds, those black eyes staring blankly into mine. Whether dead or alive, it was a sight I didn't want to see. God, to see him dangling from a branch? Or with slit wrists hunched and vulture-eaten in a creek... What am I doing, God? What am I thinking paddling out into the darkness in the middle of the night? I don't have a clue whether Jordan left the canoe for me, or for someone else. He never strung more than ten words together at a time.

His mother is supposed to come and get his stuff later this week after we get back from the break. I don't know. It's just weird to me that just like that everyone assumes he's dead, or never coming back, and that it's time to start returning to the camp normal. I don't know what I'm saying. What else are we supposed to do? He shot a gun in the air and disappeared into the woods, into country that stretches for hundreds of miles and has no shortage of abandoned barns and hundred-year-old lean to's and wretched houses that haven't been lived in since the Land Run, and we don't know where he is. He can't survive in the woods, and he can't seriously think he can come back to camp, slip into Jenni's office, and ask for a redo. Jenni is all about second chances, though. To a fault, maybe, she is all about the grace of God. It's why we all flock to her when she walks in the room. She's like this young matriarch with grace pouring out of her coffee brown eyes, and you can hear it in her laugh, and see it in her quiet moments when she's hunched over her tomato plants in solitude. But that doesn't mean she could simply take back a prodigal guy like Jordan and put him back to lifeguarding just like that. No, if he came back, he would be going straight to the courthouse. So why would he come back?

I didn't tell Lorrie that I went out last night. She just came into the cafeteria with her thermos full of coffee but is sitting a few tables behind me away from the windows, reading her Bible, kneading her forehead as she pores over the book we've always been told has all the answers to everything if you just read it hard enough.

I've been going through Ecclesiastes. It's an interesting book. One of those that sort of surprises you, almost like it doesn't fit into the Bible all that well. But the more I read it the more it feels pretty spot on. It's not like I started reading about the meaninglessness and vanity of life since Jordan's little escapade; I didn't catch it from him, so to speak. It is pretty obvious that keeping a journal, even when you don't delve too far into your strongest hopes and fears, forces you to at least think a little bit harder about life and death, and makes you wonder if thinking about much else is sort of a trivial game. Ecclesiastes is one of those books that if you encountered it in a PDF form on Academia, you might think it was written by a depressive PhD student at Harvard who had everything coming to him but suddenly stopped in his tracks on a Cambridge bridge realizing that pursuing all this stuff was a total moot point. Nada.

I like science, in case you were wondering, Professor Snodgrass, because I like observing living things, figuring out how they work. I want to see the systematics of nature, and whether indeed it has a system. It makes you wonder about the typical quandaries of life, including of course, the God question—if this stuff was designed or mindlessly evolved, and if the former, why, and if the latter, how, but it's only now that I'm off the college grind and waiting for a letter from OU and living in a tin dorm room in the woods that it has occurred to me that all this is going to end someday.

I used to think that when you write in a journal, you hold nothing back. Nothing filtered like in ordinary conversation. But here I am trying to sound smart for my creative writing class that's already over. Who am I really writing to, in the end? These words have to be based on something I really felt, and saw, and touched, or else I think I'll fail the assignment even if the letter grade is at the helm of the alphabet.

I don't know, God. Show me the way. I go from prayer to memory to fear to guilt. I guess I just pray you'd protect that poor kid, Jesus. Don't let him die, God. And if he wanted me to come after him, then maybe I'm the answer to that prayer. I'm the one who showed him the stupid gun.

He can still turn up. He can change his life. Isn't that what this is all supposed to be about, anyway?

June 8th

I went up to the office before we headed out for the long break. Jenni wasn't at the desk, but Jordan's journal still lay next to her closed laptop, strapped closed with an elastic band. There are all these stickers on it. A weathered brown guitar. A peace sign. A skull. A thin, golden cross.

I wonder if Jenni has read any of it. Or if she kept it from the cops so Jordan's mother could have it. I wasn't sure. But I picked it up and stared at its cover for a few seconds, toying with the elastic strap that kept it closed and wondering what he wrote in there. My heart pounded. It was so quiet. I opened up the journal and it felt like breaking a sacred promise, or like Jordan was watching me from the corner of the room.

It was about half full, but he had written hardly any words. He had filled the pages with sketches, doodles, and full-blown pictures. They were good, too. Faces of tigers. Lots of guitars, and a few scandalous ones of anime-style females, I'll admit.

My hands were sweating when I got to the last page, where I found, kid you not, a drawing of what looked like me sitting at the edge of the dock, head bowed like I was writing something down, with a canoe in the foreground. On the page next to it, he'd written in skeletal, childlike penmanship:

Here at this place Camp Woodward.

I don't know anybody.

Nobody knows me, either. Everybody feels phony. Giving me looks. Girls whispering about me. Welcome back to junior high.

I don't know what to say or do.

The dude Hunter is all right, idk. He told me to get off my phone, and nobody's ever told me that except teachers, but he didn't mean anything by it. Maybe he's all right.

I wonder if anyone will come looking for me when I'm gone.

I don't know how to journal. This is stupid. Why are they making me do this?

Should've brought my guitar. I think Hunter maybe plays, too. He said he canoes, too. Or did, once. I don't know. I haven't been in a stupid canoe since I went with Dad that one time. Whatever. I don't care.

I put the book back on the desk. Jenni walked in. She asked what I was doing but I just stood there with my knuckles on her desk, feeling some kind of way. How do I explain it? His saying I was "all right" was like his version of declaring his love for me.

"Hunter?" Jenni put her hand on my shoulder, but I didn't turn around. "Hunter. You didn't look in that book, did you?"

"He kept a journal. Sort of. Just like me!" I tried to laugh.

"Lots of people keep journals, buddy."

"You told me to look after him. Keep an eye on him."

"Oh man. Don't do this to yourself. I knew you would do this to yourself." Jenni made me face her and settled her hands on my shoulders. "There are some things that nobody can see coming, okay? I thought we had all summer to try and help Jordan. It was going to take a while to warm the waters and get him to come out of his shell. Turns out we only had two weeks, not even that. But listen, NO ONE knew what he was going to do, and it was NOT your fault. Do you understand me?" She gripped my shoulders extra hard when she annunciated "stand" in "understand." She wasn't messing around. It was almost like how I responded to that moment, to her words, would define the trajectory of the summer, and maybe even the whole year, and maybe even my whole life. "If anything it's *my* fault. I hired Jordan. I took a chance on someone I didn't know very much about. Okay?" All I understood in that moment, though, was that without me, Jordan would have never found the gun. A simple fact of the matter.

June 11th

Back at home.

I totally forgot that Mom and Dad were going to New York for the week for vacation. They're going to see the *Lion King* on Broadway and see an old friend who is now a divorcee and works in Manhattan as a failed playwright, or something.

They've been planning this trip for seven months and I just totally up and forgot about it. Given everything that's happened though, that doesn't seem too crazy. Last conversation I had with Mom she even said they'd fly back right away, but I said no, that would be pointless.

Lorrie and I went to Sonic on the way into town and went to the park to drink our slushies in silence on one of the old concrete tables at the top of the hill overlooking the lake. It was pretty hot, and the sidewalks are under construction this summer so we didn't walk around the lake, and we didn't know what to say to each other. We still haven't talked about *us,* or had the "talk," or whatever you call that awkward, threatening conversation that will either curse or verify the relationship. After Jordan ran away, she spent a lot of time with Jenni in Jenni's house. I ambled by the gravel road, eyeing the rec field and the water jug and its apropos tent above it, where I thought I met God and where Jordan tried to shoot at Him, while Jenni and Lorrie sat at the kitchen table and *talked.* Then she spent a lot of time in the common area in the dorms with the other girls, more listening than pitching in; I haven't seen her cry since the dock where she begged me not to go into the woods to look for Jordan, and I didn't tell her, or anybody else for that matter, that I did go out into the blackness amid the cicadas and creeping snakes, never used the flashlight, and rowed back to the dock feeling stupid and afraid, and sprinted back to the dorms up the hill around 1 a.m.

She looked tired, with her hair was ruffled and clumped around her shoulders, and I suggested she go home and take a nap and get a good night's sleep and then maybe we could hang out once we're both feeling a bit more rested, or whatever. It was easier blaming our lack of communication on sleepiness. We were both shell shocked, to tell the truth.

But she said okay, that would be good. When she dropped me off, it proceeded to occur to me that my parents were gone, along with their little Impala, leaving me carless and with no apparent way into the house.

Turns out, though, that it wasn't hard to break in. I used the grip from the palms of my hands to raise the window in the garage, and folded my body inside to rejoicingly discover the spare key in its promised little safe that hangs on a peg over Dad's workbench, and there you go: I got into the house.

Mom had left a note on the counter, laying out inventory. She bought pizzas, ramen noodles, and a massive box of assorted chips. Dad had abandoned the rest of the coffee beans into my care in the postscript, noting, as if I had never ground coffee before, that these beans were *whole* but that the grinder was on the counter by the toaster and the coffeemaker was a-okay and ready to go. The living room was neat and shadowy. The old books on the shelves in the corner bespoke their wisdom in louder voices that usual. I was hungry and fatigued after the slushie, and examined the freezer for the pizza, of which I found five stacked on each other, and popped it into the oven, cracking open a ginger beer and sitting at the kitchen table to look at the birds in the backyard.

I checked the local and state news. There were several headlines but most of them were from around four days ago, reporting that the "18-year-old man" had not been found, confounding the local authorities and stoking the need for the state law enforcement to get involved. Strange. A total enigma. It was like he vanished into thin air and riddled his way trans-dimensionally down to Juarez, or El Paso, or Dallas. I tossed away the phone and ate the pizza alone in my bedroom chair. It felt like a long day of lab work, group projects, and final exams had just quit me but still left a residue of dread and deadlines. Like I said, I don't think anyone really wanted to leave camp for good after the incident. The world outside camp wasn't anymore reassuring. For me, at least. Jordan couldn't have known where I lived. He isn't going to come knocking on my door and confess that I was the only kid at Camp Woodward he can feel like he can talk to, and wonder if he can lay low here a few days and lay out a plan. Further plans for escape, I guess? Once you accomplish one getaway you have to arrange the rest of your life to accommodate living on the lam.

Around six I went down to the Green River, the spring fed channel that runs along banks of red clay for about sixty miles. It's another dry summer. I walked across cracked and mud-stained ground to get to the healthy vein of running water. The pool at the foot of the falls swirled and eddied and flung its current after a couple of revolutions. I took off my shirt and shorts and slipped in wearing just my briefs, dunking my head under the white shaft of waterfall and letting myself sink down to the bottom, grazing the muddy floor with my eyes closed. The gentle roar of the falls and the cold, mirthful current on my head tousled my hair like a great-grandfather who has forgotten everything except how to delight in his descendants. I burst out and flopped upon the bank of grass on the other side when the sound of car wheels crunched up the gravel driveway beyond the knoll and two doors opened up after the engine stopped.

It had to be the parents. Surely they had a change of heart in the Dallas airport, kneading their hospitable hands and thinking of their son back home who had just experienced the most exciting and disturbing incident of his life. I pattered through the shallows and gathered my clothes on the rocks, not bothering, for some reason, to slip even the shorts back on as I tacked my way through a layer of woods and announced myself on the lawn. Carey and her new husband Jared were walking hand in hand up to the front door.

Carey saw me first as Jared, who, his wedding day excepted, unequivocally wears an OU baseball cap and sunglasses and shin length cargo shorts, carried their duffel bag through the front door and called out, "Hey coach, where ya at?"

I stood in the sun, wet and shading my eyes, looking back at my sister, who cocked her head and gave a lopsided grin that suggested she had just vaulted back in time ten years when she used to wrangle me in from the creek to come and get dinner. For some affectionate reason we'll call relief I didn't explain myself but stood there in the mostly nude as she scampered down the porch steps.

"Thought we'd come by for a few days," she said. It occurred to me that I hadn't seen Carey since her wedding day, and that by surmising the jammed timeline in my head, she and Jared had just gotten back from their honeymoon and had chosen to forego the move in date to their apartment in the city and camp out at the parent-less homestead for a week. "Mom told me you'd be holed up here for a few days."

"I forgot they were leaving, somehow," I said, smiling.

"You going to dry off?"

"That was the plan. Sorry I'm not *decent*. I just took a quick dip. Didn't get here too long ago, actually. How was Costa Rica?"

"Oh my gosh, amazing! We'll tell you about it inside. But hey. I heard about what happened."

Carey doesn't generally call or text me to catch up with her. When we're together, though, she gets me to herself in a corner and leans forward with her elbows on her thin running legs, lopsidedly smiling and bopping my forehead so I'll give all the details of my life heretofore. But that day she wrapped me up all wet and smelling of livid tree frog and trout and tugged at my hand up the front steps as Jared reappeared duffel-less with his sunglasses perched on the bill of his hat.

"Coach!" he said. I don't know why he calls me that. Jared is a cool guy, deserving, I'd cautiously say, of my big sister, and has always managed that superfluous enthusiasm just when I would figure it would expire, like gas in a large tank. He clapped me on the arm and asked if I minded them crashing in my "crib" for a few days, and I said not at all, I was glad for the company and frankly hadn't a notion at all of what I was going to do with the time off. Having time off from Camp Woodward is like, in the best possible spin, getting discharged from a prison after being there for thirty years. You've adapted your mind to a particular world, a certain enclosure of being, so that the rest of what apparently is supposed to be the world too seems almost vulnerable to the touch, like you're not supposed to be there. I didn't tell that to Jared, though. I just said it was nice to have a few days off.

Carey went out again and brought in a couple bags of groceries and introduced a frozen pizza that she said would be perfect for dinner that night, and I went upstairs to shower while they unloaded the goods into the pantry.

I hadn't even been in my room yet. The door to the attic was slightly askew, and I went inside it for a moment to observe those thin reams of evening light that seep up from the eaves. My little writing desk, or whatever you want to call that makeshift office, sat in the corner with a Bible and a copy, for whatever reason I couldn't quite recall, of *The Adventures of Huckleberry Finn* by Mark Twain. I picked up the book, still in underwear, and flipped through the yellow-edged pages. I heard my sister and brother-in-law downstairs, putting things away, the makeshift parents who are way, way too kind to me. Why is everyone being so kind to me?

June 12th

Today was church. And a lot more, I might add.

I woke up at eight in the morning and lay looking at the ceiling for a few minutes, then got up and went downstairs in sweatpants and a tank top, intending on unearthing Dad's infinite coffee supplies. Something barked in the backyard. A shiny red Australian shepherd bounded through the grass and snapped up a frisbee thrown by Jared, hanging five feet in the air with the grace of a ballerina. Carey ran up to the dog and rubbed its happy jowls, then snatched the frisbee and ran around the backyard with the pup bounding at her heels and yipping for a repetition. Jared, of course, already made coffee. He drinks more than Dad, and that's saying something. I got a mug and leaned against the fridge, watching my sister and brother-in-law play in the backyard like children at eight in the morning.

They came in huffing with ruddy faces flushed with exercise. Carey said they picked up Gracie, the dog, the day after they got back from Costa Rica via a desperate acquaintance who was moving to a no-pet apartment complex in Dallas.

Carey asked if I wanted some breakfast, and I told her I was going to cook some eggs or something, but she replied, "Nonsense, idiot. I'm cooking for both of you. Pancakes!"

I remember when she used to do this just about every Sunday morning. Pronouncing dominion over the breakfast table, resurrecting the tin pot from under the counter and burying her hands in flour so it bloomed atomically in her face. I sat down with my coffee and pet the dog, who had come in smiley-eyed and panting to lick my feet. Jared apologized for that, but I laughed and said no worries, that I like dogs and that it's been a while since I've had one around that actually liked me.

Despite the happy banter, the restlessness from the last few days made all these graces falter at the gate. Jordan towered behind the barriers. Those final lines from his sketchbook journal staring point blank at me in all the "you're a good kid" and "I'm making you pancakes" and the laughing Green River that also tried to wash me over with sanctification. I just haven't been able to sit still since reading those lines. Of course, I bet the authorities will want to read it, although they won't find any dark elaborate plans in there—just a few peripheral sketches of bears, serpents, and randomly, yours truly, hunched on the dock in apparent meditative devotion. Did he really want to be my friend? *Me?* The one who suddenly transformed into an ancient curmudgeon in his presence, worse than a boomer at Thanksgiving? *You're actually not allowed to have your phone,* or whatever petty thing I'd said to him at the waterfront.

After the pancakes and another round of coffee, we debated cordially about whether to go to church that morning. It would require of us the heinous inconvenience of putting on starchy pants and Baptist pastels, and a sundress for Carey, as well as the awkward condolences and wide-eyed inquiries from all the congregants who had surely heard about the incident at Camp Woodward. I didn't want the attention. It wasn't *me* they should be looking for, or praying for, or worrying for. There's a lot of overlap with people who go to my church and camp. Most of the staffers go to the church here themselves. I didn't know what I was supposed to say to them. Jordan *wasn't* a bad kid. He had a gun and he could've done some real damage, yes, but he *didn't use it,* and is it really all that shocking that someone of his rejectable caliber was on that kind of brink?

"We don't have to go if you don't want to," said Carey. "Jared and I thought about going, but only because we really haven't been in a few weeks because of the wedding. I think we're feeling prepared for all the 'how was your honeymoon' questions, aren't we hon?"

"I will never be ready for that," said Jared. "What business is it of theirs? What are we supposed to say? We had sex like twenty-eight times. That's how it was. It was awesome."

I spit coffee out at that, and Carey punched him brutally on the collarbone so I thought the man's appendage might snap, but he only recoiled with a chortle and made quick penance.

"Excuse this moron's table manners, little brother," she said. "You see why *he* needs to go to church. Total pagan sinner."

"I'll go," I said. "We don't get Sundays off at camp. I need to go."

"A Christian camp that doesn't get Sundays off," said Carey, shaking her head. "Haven't they read Genesis?"

We got ready in our separate rooms. I hadn't brought much out to camp, so found my tightly folded raw denim jeans in the bottom drawer and put on a plaid long-sleeved button down that hid the sunburn on my forearms. It felt like I was going to a funeral. Like everyone was going to overwhelm me with their concerned expressions and shoulder pats and side hugs. I'm good at smiling the part when necessary. I'm good at telling Mom's friends that I'm hoping to go to OU med school and endure the toil of a residency thereafter, for the security, you see, the monetary security of it all.

Jared and Carey are taking the ping pong room, which is lingo for the room that was originally intended to be an attic but is now a hot game room with a short ceiling. And we drove to First Baptist Church on 16th street in Jared's Ford Focus, playing the Christian radio station, and all the while I was starting to get all clammy with sweat, and another case of the thundering heartbeats.

We got there a little bit late, which was fine by me, and went upstairs and sat at the back of the balcony while the worship band sang "All Creatures of Our God and King," which is one of my favorites, but it took me a while to warm up to it. I kept looking around at everyone, even though I couldn't see many people's faces, and looked at Pastor Bill at the front pew down below. He had his hands in his pockets and was looking at the ground, sort of mumbling the words as they were sung, but like he had his mind on something else. He always sort of looked like that during the service. Like he was thinking more about what he was going to say up until the very last second before he had to say it. He, like everyone else, knows that I am the nice Saint kid, who never stirs up any trouble and who is probably going to go to OU medical school in the fall and do all right for himself, and is going to find a fine Baptist church somewhere up there and maybe marry Lorrie if she will have me. I don't know why I'm writing so cynically, Professor Snodgrass. It's not right. But I don't feel right.

After the worship was over and Bill got up there at his podium, splaying his Bible out and putting his hands back in his pockets, the screens behind him revealed that we would be hearing about the parable of the lost sheep.

It's a beautiful parable. Arguably the most beautiful parable in the whole canon. Here's this shepherd with a glorious flock somewhere off the mountain of Gilead, an even hundred, but he's so meticulous, he's so flawlessly attuned to his flock, that he notices the very instant one of them goes missing. And he hunts it in the woods. Into the frightening dark woods where bears and snakes and vines grow wild, immune from civilization.

"You know, sometimes we see certain people go off in a bad way, and we don't go after them," said Bill. "We tell them we love them, maybe, and that we want the best for them, but when they fall off the wagon, so to speak, or start making us uncomfortable by their behavior, well, then we just let them alone, figuring that's the best we can do for them. Just let them alone, never thinking to intervene, point them in the right direction." Carey must've noticed how much I was sweating and shaking because she put her kind, kind hand on my leg and whispered if I was all right, but I was terrible, and replied with nothing but a clenched jaw. "We need to be more attentive. I'd bet anything that there's a person in *your* life that you could be witnessing to, that God has personally *put* in your life, but that you're avoiding, or that you failed in some way. It's not right. The Lord deserves better. He called you to more. We are *called* to share the gospel…of Jesus Christ."

To make it a double whammy, another slide came up on the screen. It was a screenshot of a New York Post headline, of all things, showing the high school portrait of none other than Jordan himself, smiling with one side of his mouth, producing one dimpled chin, with his hair only long enough to cover his ears. He was such a baby. *OKLAHOMA BOY FIRES GUN AT KIDS' CAMP AND VANISHES.*

"Now I know a lot of you have heard about what happened over at Camp Woodward this past week. A terrible thing. Something that never should have happened, frankly. But I want you to look into this young man's eyes." I did. I looked very hard. "And I want you to ask yourself something. If this young man was your son, or your brother, or even your cousin, would you help him when he got in trouble? Would you put a roof over his head if he didn't have a place to stay? Would you share the gospel to him if he wasn't a believer? I know I'm going to get a lot of angry emails for this one, but listen, folks, I have to ask it: would you *love* this troubled young man? God does. And he's calling you to think of that person in your life today and to *go* to them in the name of Jesus, to declare truth and repentance to them, and to not *put it off* one day longer. Otherwise, look what happens." He pointed at the picture. At what happens.

That final spiel got a round of "amens" so potent that I heard it even as I swung the door open to the men's room and sat inside the single stall in the corner.

I sat there rubbing my hands on my raw denim thighs, pulling out my phone and opening Jenni's texting tab. What did I have to say to her? Nothing. There was no escape from this.

The door opened a couple of minutes later. Someone shuffled in and stopped, and by the silence and the stationary tennis shoes, I surmised that the someone wasn't going to be using the bathroom. It was Jared. "What do you say, Coach? You all right? You seemed a little bit rattled."

I tried to reply to him. I did. I look up to Jared a lot when it's all said and done. I always wanted a big brother. Sometimes it felt like I was surrounded by mainly women growing up—sweet women, mind you, women who loved God and loved me and were always so *kind* to me, but Jared being in the mix was a good thing, you know. I tried to say that I was fine, that this was just the morning pancakes kind of doing a number to me, but all I managed was a kind of pathetic wheeze that communicated precisely the opposite. "Hey chief, it's all right." Jared was quiet again and then added, "Hunter, I know you're upset about what happened at camp. Geez, man, I can't imagine. Seeing that kid shoot the gun and run off, not knowing if he was ever going to come back."

"I don't think he's coming back," I said, pressing my elbows against my thighs and bowing my head so my lengthening hair flipped out over my brow. "Why would he come back? Nobody talked to him. I bet nobody talked to him his old stupid life."

Jared shuffled again. He cleared his throat and sounded like he rubbed his stubbly chin. In the quiet, Pastor Bill's voice made it through the thin walls of the men's room.

"It's okay," he told me. "You couldn't have done anything about it, man. That kid was *troubled*. He wasn't in a good position to work there. He should've been getting help."

To this, I had nothing to say. I love Jared, but what was I supposed to say back? Jenni hired Jordan for the kid's own benefit—and she told me, *me*, to befriend him. That was the person God had put in my life to help. I had my clique with Zach and Lorrie and the twins. I was the beneficiary of Jenni's attention. I was content with being a veteran who comfortably knew the ropes of this small Baptist village in the curtains of backwoods Oklahoma and didn't need an anomaly like Jordan to stir the pot.

"We're here for you, Hunter," said Jared. "All right? We're always here for you."

When he left, and I was still constipated in rump and spirit, I had the strange wish for someone to be angry at me. Like actually sort of furious. I live in a town and a church and a family that says practically nothing to your face. I only realized this when I went off to college and met a couple of northerners. There was a British girl in my micro class who used to bluntly call me a clueless American on occasion, but you could tell that she didn't mean anything by it—it was just how she was, and then she would slap me on the arm and tell me to buck up.

I used to think the wrath of God in the Old Testament (and the New, upon further inspection) could be pretty harsh. I wondered how God's anger fit with his love, and how God *is* love, like it says in 1st John 4. And it still confounds me to a degree, to be honest, but the longer I'm around, the more I'm a bit dissatisfied with the one-sided kind of love that smiles in your face but never smacks you upside the head when you need it. I'm not saying I need it right now. Maybe I do. And I'm not saying it would be welcome from just any old joe on the street. But say Carey, for instance—if she were to corner me and put a finger at my forehead and stare at me with wide, furious eyes, I'd take it seriously. After she was done yelling at me, I'd go off raw but real, like I had just been brought back to the world after parading in my own la-la land for a few days.

Revelation 19 starting in verse 12 goes like this:

> "His eyes are a flame of fire, and on His head are many diadems; and He has a name written on Him which no one knows except Himself. He is clothed a robe dipped in blood, and His name is called the Word of God. And the armies which are in heaven, clothed in fine linen, white and clean, were following Him on white horses. From His mouth comes a sharp sword, so that with it He may strike down the nations, and He will rule them with a rod of iron; and He treads the wine press of the fierce wrath of God, the Almighty. And on His robe and on His thigh He has a name written, KING OF KINGS, AND LORD OF LORDS."

For all those allergic to tattoos, note that the warrior Christ has one stamped on his thigh, and this one really *means* something. But suppose you actually *saw* that on your way to the supermarket. A blazing Man upon a horse with an army in the millions forming a sea behind, stretching back pretty much forever.

And then I just kept sitting there thinking about that. Wishing someone would be mad at me. I want weird things, sometimes, and I know for a fact none of this would make sense if I tried to say it to someone. Problem is, people get mad at other people mainly because their egos get ruffled, or their sensitivity is offended, or something such. It's rarely, from my point of view, very rarely, because one fellow has genuine heartfelt concern for the other.

One time, Zach had this thing with a girl. She actually worked at Camp Woodward a couple of years ago, and that's how they met, but she went to school in Arkansas. They dated long distance for a little while before it fell apart.

But he kept being on again and off again with her. Breaking up with her over text and then calling to apologize. That sort of nonsense. For a guy who typically speaks his mind, it was like he just couldn't stick with her for more than a week or so, and he was constantly morbid about it and moping around the dorm room running his hand through his mullet and listening to some godawful Nickleback or something such, and it got to the point where I couldn't take it anymore, and I said in the nicest way possible something like, "Hey bro, you gotta choose. Eventually, you know, I think you just need to commit to her or make sure that you're just friends. You're stringing her along just to cut her loose, and that's not right." It was a day or two later that I realized it was the most confrontational thing I ever said. Which probably indicates that I'm a pretty passive and chill guy most of the time. Why people call me "Saint" as a nickname.

But I'd like to think it was because I care about the guy. He's my best friend and I didn't want to see him so miserable and go on with this gaping moral blind spot, and the girl, Sarah, always seemed nice to me. Zach didn't take it too well at first, but the next day we were sitting in the lobby of the Baptist Student Union with our sweet teas when he said, "I appreciate you saying that stuff yesterday. I talked to Sarah this morning. We both agreed that it's over. It sucks. But it's good. I'm sad but at peace, if that makes any stupid sense."

It does make stupid sense. Sucks but it's good. Sad but at peace. I get that. I sincerely do.

But here's the crazy part. When we got back home from church, I went up to my room and jotted this stuff down, but then without skipping a beat I pulled out my old mountain pack from behind a box of Christmas decorations and stuffed my single-man tent, sleeping bag, and .22 pistol inside. Then I snuck downstairs and gathered a bunch of apples and tomato soup cans and stuffed those in the pack too while Jared and Carey spoke on the phone to the parents up in the game room. I grabbed a handful of clothes and changed into some loose jeans and my tank top, fastened on my Camp Woodward ball cap, and slipped out the backdoor into the woods. *Woodward*, if you will.

Going to find the lost sheep.

June 13th

It's morning. I camped last night next to the Green River about five miles downstream from home. I found a power line where they paved an opening through the woods, and traveled down it for most of the day, searching the ground for tracks, or some other sign of him. Now I can hear the water trickling just through the trees.

I didn't bring my phone. Not sure if that was intentional or not. Probably wasn't the wisest move, honestly.

The plan here is simple: walk the forty-odd miles from home to Camp Woodward in search of the lost boy, or really any signs of him that he might have left. Fortunately for me, the Green River flows out of the lake at Camp Woodward, or at least, one of the thick channels makes a tributary to the Green River. Follow that all the way and you're right at Camp Woodward's doorstep.

There hasn't been a sign of him. Nothing but a strand of deer tracks and the remains of an old shack, which I entered only to find the burnt remains of a bedspring and piles of rotting insulation. It was so hot in there, and so old and chemically smelling, that I stumbled out pressing my face in my shirt.

I wanted to set up the tent close to the water so there would be some white noise in the night. I still don't even know exactly what I'm doing— Lorrie's voice is in my ear, reminding me that if state troopers couldn't find him, then there was little chance of *my* finding him, even for someone who grew up in the woods and sort of knows what to look for when in search of a blundering eighteen-year-old kid. But when the night set in, the adrenaline wore off, and there was no coffee in the mountain pack, the urge to trek back home was overpowering. Plus, Carey would be worried stiff. She's even worse than Mom with that kind of stuff. I made the tent near the river, but left the tarp off, and lay on my back on top of the sleeping bag in nothing but boxers. The tree branches crowded out most of the sky, but streaks of purple and orange made a background, preparing the infinite darkness behind it, like someone hugging you before leaving off for a great war. I was hungry, got a bad headache, and slipped my headlamp on without turning it on. It got to feeling like the other night when I went off in the canoe and got scared witless over shining the flashlight into the woods. It's not darkness anybody fears. At the end of the day, I fear the light and what a concentrated dose of it might reveal. But the sounds of the river, Grandfather River's happy rushing over stones and against banks of clay, along with the hush of locusts, and a third thing that maybe amounted to Carey's prayers, helped me drift off to sleep.

June 14th

If I walk ten miles a day, I'll be at Camp Woodward before the next camp comes in and business resumes as usual. By then, the staff will probably be pacified, the local authorities will no longer be intrigued with pressing charges against this boy who many probably now believe to be imaginary, and Zach and I will fish on the dock and only casually wonder where Jordan ended up. Mexico? Canada? More modestly—Oklahoma City, Dallas/Ft. Worth metro-plex? Did he have anyone to go to besides his mother?

Writing this in the evening. On the verge of forgetting what day it is. And it's harder to write now that there's no table to write on. I'm using the mountain pack as a makeshift.

I walked alongside the river all day. Eventually I'll need to cross it, if my mental geographics are serving me right. It's a deep river in some places. It has all these terraces where small waterfalls lap over into green pools, which drop off into more pools. The current runs thicker and stronger next to the grassy banks in certain spots, flooding over shallow receipts of shale and granite. I've already swum in it twice, and climbed a willow tree overhanging a deep, shady part of the river.

About midday I got out of the woods and into a stretch of prairie. I stopped and ate two apples and some blackberries from a bush, and then walked on a sort of grassy crag overlooking the river, where it curved somewhat east and narrowed beneath a canopied tunnel of oak and elm trees. I went down close to the water again, finding a shallow stretch, took off my sneakers, and waded upstream. I kept dipping my blue bucket hat into the water and putting it back on again.

I went under Highway 3, where swallow nests line the bridge's underbelly and the birds flit and skitter like crazy pilots, and about a half a mile past the bridge, found another spot in the woods where it looked like a lot of deer bedded down at night, flattening the grass. I built my tent here and am now writing and hungry and hot. I think of Carey and Jared and what they must think of me right now. It was really stupid of me to leave without saying anything, and even stupider for not taking my phone with me—but if I had run into them on the way out they would have convinced me not to go. And I probably wouldn't have wanted to go, and I don't think I even want to be here now. That's what really haunts me, journal, or my reflected conscience as seen in these pulpy sketchbook pages: I don't think I actually want to find Jordan. I wouldn't know what to do if I did.

June 15th

The first piece of evidence uncovered today. At around nine in the morning, I reached a deep, lazy part of the Green River, and saw a canoe tipped upside down in the shallows on the other side, its tan, fiberglass stitched underbelly unmistakably marking it as the property of Camp Woodward. I hurled the pack down on the bank and stripped to my shorts, then swam through the slow-moving current until staggering up on the other side. The boat was cradled in some cattail reeds, completely upside down. I had to reach underneath the lip of the boat, feeling its wooden trim, and hoisted the thing up with some considerable effort, feet plugged into the clay, until it flipped right side up and steadied, so it didn't catch any current. Water sloshed down the sides, producing a single bloated tennis shoe that surfaced then went underneath again in its waterlogged dead-weight. I snatched the shoe, wary of snakes, pouring the water out of it and inspecting it to find that it was a loose laced Nike tennis shoe, totally black save for the red swoosh on its side. Jordan's boat, and Jordan's shoe. Grunting and gasping, I hauled the canoe ashore and tossed the shoe back in, and then peered up and down the river, behind me, and even up in the trees, as if he might be watching me soundlessly from a hidden branch.

"Jordan?" I kind of shouted. The sound of my own voice made my skin crawl for some reason. Like it belonged to someone else. But I said it again, a little louder with my hands cupped at my mouth. "Jordaaaan!"

Birds tittered in the trees and a rabbit bounded through the tall grass, slipping through some briars and drawing my attention a few yards beyond the bank, where there was a meadow buzzing with gnats and tree frogs. A couple of vultures shuddered in the dead branches of some persimmon tree, eyeing something. Oh, God no, I was thinking to myself. I didn't want to have to go back and get my clothes, since they'd get wet in the crossing, so I found a narrow path used most likely by the deer and tiptoed towards the meadow in my bare feet. I kept calling his name, bending my head to check my step and then up again to check out the area around me, feeling like an idiot and totally vulnerable in these sopping boxers—I'm already out of underwear so I guess this is my version of laundry out here.

It didn't really come to anything, this escapade, despite the vultures. I thought maybe he'd be somewhere in the meadow, foraging for berries, or maybe sleeping, but once I got there all I saw was this dead coyote draped across a low hanging branch in a bodark tree. A cloud of flies flurried the carcass, and the stench was bad even from where I was standing. It was weird. It gave me an odd feeling. That was what the vultures were eating.

In any case I spent most of the afternoon poking around the meadow, and then got tired around three, and so took a nap on a long rock next to the water.

I wondered who killed the coyote, thinking about it when the sun was setting and the locusts were going crazy again, and the canoe and its shoe lay dried and tidy on the bank.

June 16th

Don't know what to make of the boat and the shoe.

Clearly he used the canoe until it flipped. He probably jumped ship, lost the shoe in the melee, and started hiking with a bare foot. I don't want to think about the other option. There is no other option. He's still out here.

Thinking about Lorrie this morning. Wonder if she's heard that I'm missing. Also, Jenni. Jenni probably figured what I was up to already. Lorrie would probably guess it, too. But thinking about the family with Mom and Dad in New York and Carey and Jared at the house is sort of killing me. I woke up this morning and skinny dipped in the river and then sat on the edge of a six-foot-tall waterfall with my bare back to the current like I was in a fancy hot tub with the jet stream flooding against me. I sat there for a good while looking up at the morning sky and trying to pray, remembering for a second when I had that experience by the water jug in the rec field, and how that night felt like years ago now, almost delegated to another lifetime. It felt good to sit on the edge of the waterfall with the roar of the water in my ears, drowning everything else out. I still thought about Lorrie. If she was worried about me or not. Stupid, immature thoughts like that. But I have them.

I feel bad. Carey and Jared came back from their honeymoon to stay with me for the two weeks of off-time, and the first morning of their stay I up and vanished without explanation. It wasn't right. I know that, God. Something about the sermon at church, alongside the notion that if I don't try and do this *now* it will be completely too late, alongside the further no-tion that to prove my devotion to saving the lost sheep entrusted in my care I *needed* to do this. That if I didn't at least try, it would mean I didn't care about Jordan, which meant I didn't care about lost people, which meant I just maybe wasn't a child of God to begin with.

The more I have these thoughts the less I'm able to sleep. I stopped writing a few minutes ago but am back at it again.

How far away is camp? It's hard to say. My sense of time and direction is starting to blur. Also, the food supply is totally supped. Nada. I had the last bit of apple today and scoured the campsite for berries, but all I found was a massive bush of honeysuckle. You should have seen it, Prof. Lorrie would have loved it. Carey and Jenni, too. Maybe I'm going a little coo-coo out here and have to pretend that this journal is sentient and can nod along to my quackeries. But anyway, the honeysuckle. The plant wrapped around a massive sycamore tree and extended its fronds over a crown of thorns, with its hundreds of open buds looking like tiny trumpets, each with their own special little note to sing. Man, it was a really lovely sight. The sun shining right through the sycamore branches and flooding on the honeysuckle buds. Times like that sometimes make me wonder if nature itself is sort of sentient. Or has an idea of the kind of wonder it produces in the world. But then I remember that it's all God's creation. Back to orthodox Christianity, idiot. He's the Mind behind the world. Like the stars are behind the sunsets.

It was all *His* idea in the first place. Sometimes I just wish I could hear Him speak.

June 17th

Woke up very hungry. I'm about a hundred feet away from the river. Drank some water using this little filter that I forgot was already in the mountain pack. Thank God. The Green River is mostly spring fed, but still. After breaking down camp, I set the pack aside and hunted for more black-berries. I found a big bush full of them and filled up my bucket hat so the inside of it got absolutely stained with juice, but I didn't care, and ate just about the whole crate of it.

I saw three young bucks this morning as I started the morning tramp. One of them was so young that its summer horns had just appeared. They were fuzzy adolescent nubs. The second one was a bit older with a mature, four-point rack and eyes black as glass. He was grazing near the water on the opposite shore, and raised his head to look at me as I blundered through the brush. He surprisingly didn't bounce into the trees behind him. He only observed me like I was some strange but not unwelcome new addition to the animal kingdom, and took another long drink of water.

The third one I saw had only half a rack of antlers. He must've shed the other half or lost it in a scuffle with another buck. I counted eight points on that one side. It was like a tree was growing out of his head. This time, the river was some distance to my left, and I was stepping over a couple of fallen logs when I heard his hooves press through the leaves. He wasn't grazing. He didn't stop to look at me. He walked surely and deliberately through a little group of birch trees, eyes fixed ahead of him like he was on a fated mission that was meant to go uninterrupted.

By the end of today I was so tired that I couldn't even set up camp. I found a spot right next to the water underneath a willow tree and laid out the sleeping mat on the ground. It was only until I'd settled down with the journal that I saw the morrells. A little school of the delicate mushrooms popped up beneath the eroded root system of the willow tree. These are rare to find. With my feet dunked in the shallows, I ate about seven of the twenty that were there, intending on saving the rest for tomorrow, and then laid down. I thanked God for the meal, and right before I decided to go to sleep, said in a conversational tone, "Jordan!"

As if just saying his name would bring him out of the woodwork.

June 19th

You'd think I'd be getting close. There hasn't been a road or highway since the bridge a couple days ago, and I know for a fact that the Green River ducks under another bridge and snakes through another stretch of prairie before branching off into that little creek I mentioned—the one that connects conveniently to Woodward.

Maybe I'm just making dang slow progress in the woods. We get so used to zooming around in cars and planes that walking three miles in forestry feels like a throwback to the age of Neanderthal, an age for which we are decidedly *most* unprepared!

I took the rest of the mushrooms with me and chanced upon more berries, but what would really be nice (besides a hot meal at the Woodward caf) would be a young trout grilled to perfection. I might be able to catch a trout. I'd done as much before with just a net, if you can believe it. But in all reality, the best I could do this afternoon, admittedly after throwing rocks at a passing turtle, was scavenge a school of crawdads, and came up with a pretty good sprawl.

Only problem? Either it was eat them raw or figure out some way to harness man's primordial creation: fire!

The mountain pack held no more secrets besides the water filter, which was a miracle enough; there weren't even matches in the top pocket. I did find one of Dad's ancient handkerchiefs. It's so old and has been in there so long that I could barely make out the design, but eventually decided that it's a map of Glacier National Park up in Montana. There are topographical ridges riddling across the starchy wrinkles of the fabric, and a barely visible compass whose most visible direction is a dark blue *N*, denoting North. Who knows how many miles of incalculably dense and dangerous wilderness are symbolized in this musky twenty inches of cloth. I've been wearing the thing as a bandana ever since finding it.

Weirdly enough, as I was hauling this hatful of crawdads along and feeling a bit nauseous, I guess from the terribly slim diet I've been on, the figure of a dilapidated building peered into view through the trees. It was made of stone, a rectangle in shape, with its two stories still intact but with a caved in roof. All the windows gaped freely, and what used to be the door had a couple of collapsed slats of wooden beams making a V in its open space. I cautiously approached, setting the crawdads down and peeking "inside" to find that the whole interior is overgrown with tall dense grass and small tree in its center, reaching up past the old joists that used to support the second floor, and the remains of a spiral staircase standing lopsided and termite-ridden in the corner.

I don't get the sense that this locale is a former house. Its square floor-plan and lack of any shed or other domestic remains call it into question. Upon further inspection it almost looks like a stone fortress or armory. In one of the stones a name was carved: Sue Pussycat Lansing, XOXO. Oh.

I snooped around for a little bit, although there wasn't much to see, when there right beneath the tree and half hidden with poison sumac, was the second loose laced Nike tennis shoe.

I almost bowled over, like the shoe was about to come alive and inter-rogate me with its snaky laces and demand what I was doing there, and why I'd trespassed into its comfy home. I don't usually curse but couldn't help repeating "oh shit" over and over. The canoe was one thing, and was strange enough, but this? I didn't know what to do. I snatched a lone stick and whacked through the grass like it was a scythe, reaping for more eerie clues but coming up with nothing except an upset rat snake, which slithered up the spiral staircase and observed its intruder from a height of safe repose. "Jordan!" I shouted. "Where are you man? C'mon, where are you man?" I leaped out of the old brothel or whatever the heck that place was and swept through the grass as if expecting another article of clothing to pop up and disclose to me the kid's whereabouts. I stumbled into the shallows of the river and made it to a sandbar in the middle where there was a good view of upstream and downstream. I screamed his name at the top of my lungs. My brain was reeling with blood pressure, and I fell to my bony knees sick to my stomach. I lay there on my belly for a couple hours, dehydrated and sunburnt to a crisp, with seventy-eight bug-bites up and down my legs. What's bothering me now, as I've set up camp inside the broken-down building and am so sleepy all of a sudden, is that when I get back to camp, alone, or at all, I'll have to tell Jenni, and everyone else by extension, that I found both his shoes, but not him.

June 20th

It will take a little explaining to catch things up to speed.

This morning, I woke up around six. I felt this sort of new urgency about getting to camp, and that people were actually going to start worrying for real about where I was—not that they wouldn't already be. But this morning I knew that I couldn't josh around anymore out here, and that if I was going to find Jordan at all, it would have to be during the final jaunt through the woods next to the river. And also, I dreamed about the tennis shoe. And the canoe. And then strangely, I dreamed about Lorrie walking up to the abandoned stone building in the middle of the night and peeking in through the collapsed doorframe, wearing a seamless frock sort of like they have at the hospital. She came in with her brows all knitted and her arms crossed, like she was cold, and then she just stood in the middle of overgrown parlor and looked up at the sky, then at the rotten spiral staircase, and then she took off the gown and spread herself out on the grass beneath the tree where I'd discovered the tennis shoe, her white body practically glowing in the moonlight, and I think she whispered, "Jordan, Jordan, Jordan," over and over again until I woke up feeling sick.

I dreamed later that Jordan himself walked into the old house. He kind of stumbled in, confused, with his long black hair hiding most of his face. He shone a flashlight up and down the insides of the walls and ran a gangly finger along one of the cracks from which something like a worm wriggled its translucent body and plopped, vanishing, into the grass at his feet. This dream too cast a shadow on the morning and were both so vivid and weird that I packed up the tent in five minutes and ran away from the old stone house for about two minutes straight. In the woods it was still dark, and oddly quiet, with just the soft croaking of the frogs and the thrashing of my running feet through the leaves. I ran out of breath and didn't have the energy to sustain that for too long, and so took a breather next to some old moss-covered stones by a grove of cedars, and when I looked up, an old man stared at me pointing a pistol right at my head. "Easy boy," he said, stepping sideways. He was dressed in greasy overalls and a short-sleeved white shirt that was pocked with holes and was almost as dirty as his ancient, tanned out arms, which still rippled with good muscle; his eyes were loamy brown, and he wore a cowboy hat. I don't remember what I said at first. I think I just yelled and covered my face, and then turned to the river as if it could steal me away and deliver me.

"You're on my property, boy," he said. "What you doing here?"

"Nothing, sir." The old man scowled and cocked the pistol, which apparently meant I hadn't answered the bulk of the question. I added, "I'm sorry, sir, I've been…I've been *looking* for someone." The old man straightened out, his narrowed eyes lightening a little bit, and he asked, "Who you been looking for?"

"Kid that went missing about two weeks ago. Tall white kid, long black hair. I have reason to believe that he's lost both his shoes. I found the canoe that he took off in."

"You have reason to believe he lost his shoes," the old man slowly repeated to himself, lowering the gun and scratching his chest beneath the overall strap with the barrel.

"Yes," I confirmed. "Why, you seen him? I didn't mean to trespass. Really. I'm actually headed to Camp Woodward, if you know what that is. I work there. He did too. The kid, I mean."

"Yeah, I saw him," he said, stuffing the gun in his chest pocket and replacing his trigger hand with the stub of a cigar. I lurched, clenching my hands for some reason. "You *saw* him?"

"Sure I did. Pale, nervous kid. Blundered through here during a storm the other night."

"Really? Well, where did he go? Or, did he tell you?" The old man relit the cigar with a metal lighter and stared at me while he took his first puff, then said with the thing still in his mouth, "You look shit, kid. C'mon up to the house. I'll get you some grub."

.He didn't phrase it as a request. He turned around and tramped through the woods using various trees for walking sticks, and I followed a few feet behind with no idea whether I was about to be murdered or simply walk into some nice little country home to find Jordan having apple pie and coffee. "You don't have to," I said, as tribute.

He said nothing, only swatted a low-hanging branch aside and kicked through a wall of briars, leading to a freshly excavated clearing where a beige trailer house, crusted with rain mud halfway up its sides, stood against a backdrop of foliage and hummed with an air conditioner unit. He walked directly towards a staircase and its attendant patio of unkempt wood, skirting a rusty contraption of intertangled levers and gears that best I could guess used to be some kind of plough. I heard them before seeing them, but a band of hogs grunted and wallowed in a tiny chicken wired fence attached to the left side of the house. There were four of them fighting for a trough of liquid slop, squealing the snouts distended and plowing for reward. "Pigs," I said aloud, as if to verify that I was seeing right. The old man snorted and coughed, then went up the stairs, saying, "Sorry the place is a mess."

I hesitated as he opened the door and glanced behind my shoulder, wondering if this was the last time I was going to see the daylight. What else was I supposed to do? Inside it smelled of cowboy beans, tobacco, and jerky. It smelled good. Of course, anything smells good when you're starving.

He wasn't lying. The trailer house had two compartments. The kitchen and living room were conjoined, and his bedroom was down a short hallway, but the door was closed at the end of it. A couch, worn to the threads and littered with newspapers and cigarette butts, stood against the far wall beneath the air conditioner unit, prefacing a coffee table that suffered from similar discontents.

"Sit down, if you can manage it. Chuck the papers if you need to."

I put down the mountain pack and did as I was told, sitting on the utmost edge of the couch and planting my dirty fingers on the coffee table. These papers were decades old. Some of them extolled people like Dewey and Kennedy. Reagan assassination attempt. Possible Bigfoot sighting? Crossword puzzles, mostly unfinished, joined the arrangement of language and history and time.

"Boy, you drink coffee?"

"Yes sir, I do. Thank you. It's been a few days since—"

"I don't need to know how long you been out here."

"Well. All right."

He brought a cup of instant coffee. He was heating cowboy beans on the stove, and after lighting a cigarette, sat in a dark leather recliner across from the couch so the afternoon light rippled over his thin, wiry frame. I sipped some of the coffee. It was bad, but still tasted good, somehow. Maybe because I hadn't had coffee for weeks.

"So you saw him," I said. "The kid."

"Jordan. He has a name," said the old man. "Yeah, I saw him. He sat in that exact spot two days ago."

"Yeah?" I didn't want to push him for answers too much.

"Yeah," he said. He took a long draw from the cigarette and blew it into the air, observing me with those deep brown eyes and wiping the sweat from his forehead.

"Was he all right?"

"He was fine. Had a cut on his arm. Fairly deep. We got that patched up and he was on his way. Just like that."

"Where…do you know where he was going?"

The old man flicked the ash off the end of his cigarette and held it by the armrest, letting it trail smoke as he continued to grill me with that blank austerity that somehow, at the same time, didn't feel threatening. I sipped the coffee again, glancing at the papers again for refuge, and then he said, "He said he was looking for his daddy."

He continued after a pause and a failure to respond on my part, "He said his daddy always promised they'd have some big talk on his eighteenth birthday. He said something about how it was his birthday, soon, and he couldn't be spending it working at a Christian camp in the woods. He had to go see his daddy."

"That's what he told you?" I asked.

"Along those lines."

"Did he say where his dad lived?"

The old man shook his head.

"You shouldn't look for him anymore," he said. "It's admirable that you've tried to find him. But you should give up the ghost, so to speak."

I didn't know what to say to this, either. He leaned forward with the cigarette now poised in between his teeth and extracted an ivory case knife from his back pocket. With it, he carved the excess of nail from his thumb and set the blade on the coffee table, right on top of Kennedy's assassination from 1963.

"Well. You see, we were working together over at Camp Woodward, and I didn't get much of a chance to know him all that well. But, I don't know, I felt sort of…responsible? Like I was supposed to go out and find him."

"Why you?" he asked, leaning back in his chair. The beans were beginning to bubble on the stove in the kitchen. "Why not your boss? What's her name. Jenni?"

"You know Jenni?"

"Not really. Kid mentioned her."

"She took it on herself to hire Jordan in the first place. Wanted to help him out."

"Did *he* want to be hired? That wasn't so clear to me during our conversation."

"Apparently not."

"Hmm. Well, then. All I can tell you is that he's off looking for his daddy, and he cut loose yesterday morning. There's really no telling where he is by now."

"He could be in the next county." After another sip of coffee and preponderance, I added, "Did you happen to contact the police? You know he fired a gun at camp."

"He didn't tell me about that."

"Yeah. He fired a pistol into the air in a crowd of kids and then booked it to the lakefront. He stole a canoe and floated the Green. I guess until he flipped it and found his way here."

"Sounds like an accurate description of the events, more or less." The beans boiled. The old man rose with a grunt to retrieve bowls, into which he ladled the gruel, and brought back my portion. I thanked him. He hadn't included a spoon.

"So what was your plan when you were to find him?"

"I don't know. I guess convince him to come back to camp."

"After he fired a gun into the air, where the cops and therapists and Momma and scared staffers would all be waiting."

"I guess I hadn't really thought it through. I just wanted to find him to make sure was okay."

"Boy I tell you, I ain't ever seen such a skinny kid. I gave him just about everything that would fit in his little knapsack. I even asked if he wanted to stick around a while. He was barefoot so I gave him my one spare pair of boots. They were too big for him, of course."

"He didn't tell you at all where he was going?" I asked.

The old man supped some of the beans with his fingers and licked them clean before responding. "Texas, most likely. He said his daddy went to Texas when he was ten years old. But where in Texas, he didn't seem to know."

"It's a broad target," I said. "And he stopped following the river?"

"He said he was going to follow it by foot as long as could, even though he'd lost the canoe."

It took me a few seconds to realize that by this logic, Jordan and I would have passed each other along the river. By this logic, Jordan would be passing right by my parents' house.

"You all right, son?"

"I don't know," I said, wincing and gripping the mug of coffee. "I came all the way out here, searching for him, and we probably slipped by each other without even noticing it." The old man was silent. I bowed my head now, again feeling the confessional weight of Pastor Bill's sermon on my shoulders. God, does guilt never leave us?

"It could have happened," he said. "But you never know, son. Maybe he went off another direction. Maybe he found the road and somebody gave him a ride down to Dallas." He leaned forward again, cigarette now expired, and asked me if anyone knew I was out here. I glanced at him, fearful of him a little bit again, knowing that in an alternative story he could have murdered Jordan and be about to murder me too while he was at it. But I don't know. There was something calm and timeless in his eyes. If he was ever a father, he would have been good at weeping with his children. He had that kind of eyes, if that makes any sense.

"No sir. I mean, maybe they've got a notion by now. But I didn't tell anybody where I was going."

"Why not?"

"I don't know." And honestly I still don't exactly know. Probably the reasons were practical, like I think I wrote earlier. Carey would have commandeered the efforts and I would have stayed home, which, I hate to say it, may have increased my chances of coming across Jordan ten-fold, if indeed he followed the Green River all the way to its destination.

"You ought to turn up. Tomorrow," he said. Then he noticed my lack of a spoon, and hopped up to accommodate with a brief apology. "You ain't lost, are you?"

"I don't think so. I just have to follow the river until I find the tributary that connects with Lake Woodward."

"Lots of tributaries," he said, handing me the utensil. "Especially the closer you get to the lake. Tons of little creeks bud off. All but one of 'em lead to nowhere."

"You know the woods pretty well, then?"

"I guess you could say that."

"I think I'll find it. I must be close at this point." The old man relit his initial cigar and tilted his head to the side, considering. "Yep," he agreed with a slow nod. "You're very close."

I dug into the beans with the socially acceptable spoon-method, and cleaned out the bowl in just thirty seconds. "I'll get you more," said the old man. "What's your name, son?"

"Hunter," I replied. "And thank you. I don't think I ever tasted such good beans in my life, sir."

"Anything tastes good when you're starving," he said.

After he brought me seconds, and my bites were more intermittent and less ravenous, he asked, "So what else are you looking for out here?"

"Beg your pardon, sir?"

"I said what else are you looking for out here." He said it the second time as a statement, not a question.

"Um…nothing, I guess."

"It was for Jordan and Jordan alone that you cast off civilizational constraints and took on the wilderness, eh?" I chewed on my beans for longer than necessary.

"Well, I had this experience at camp a few weeks ago," I began. I gave the room a quick investigation—as if to check for religious décor or a Bible or anything else to suggest this old man's friendliness to God. But there was no literature except for the newspapers, and no real décor besides a mounted largemouth bass above the recliner, immortalized in mid flop with its great mouth gaping and its black marble eyes retaining some of the terror of being caught.

"Go on," said the old man.

"I'm not sure what to make of it. I was out in the back field at camp filling a plastic water jug, and when I looked up at the night sky, just felt like someone was *watching* me. But not in a weird, scary way. Maybe a little bit scary." The old man placed the cigar in his mouth, left it there, and settled his brown leather hands on his knees. "So," I went on, "I think part of me is trying to have that experience again. That feeling. Like God's watching me."

"And?" said the old man through the obstacle of a cigar.

I examined the last few days in my mind. Those sleepless nights. Sitting in the waterfall. Finding the abandoned brothel. Finding the shoes and the overturned canoe. The three great bucks all so content in their solitary worlds. "I don't think so," I reported, softly, sadly. "I don't think I've ever felt so alone in my whole life, honestly."

"You're barking up the wrong tree, maybe," the old man said. "You're looking for a feeling. You had a feeling once, and it was real, and came from something real. Believe me, I've known that sensation more than a few times in my life. I don't know if it was God or a ghost or just the emanating spirit of the natural order, but it's intoxicating. I get it." He coughed, cricked his neck, and said, "But look for the feeling and you'll wind up feeling nothing at all. Except your lonesome, lonesome self. Stuck in the woods."

I glanced at him, then nodded. "Yeah. That sounds right."

"You think God's out in these woods more than He is at home? Or that He's there at camp more than he is in church?"

I considered the proposition, and said, "Yes. I really think I do."

"Got news for you." He stood up then and leaned over with his hands planted on the coffee table, covering Kennedy's assassination, and looked me level in the eyes. "God's everywhere. All the time. Every second. You know what you spend every day doing? Going from one holy spot of ground to the next. That's all anyone does every single day whether they're aware of it or not." He puffed the cigar, inducing just the least bit of a cough from my suspended lungs, and then he laughed a deep and disturbingly pure old man's laugh. "You full?" He pointed to the empty bowl resting in my hands.

"Yes sir," I whispered. "Thank you."

"All right, then." He checked his watch. "So, you'll be off now. Let me get you some apples and jerky for the road. You're very close." I stood up, taking this as the cue to leave, as he rifled through the pantry and resurrected the promised staples. "I really appreciate it, sir," I said. "Everything."

"Don't mention it. Come by again, sometime, if you're ever on another mission like this in the woods."

"Sure thing." I took the dozen or so apples and oranges he provided, as well as a couple bags of deer jerky, courtesy of the old man's hunting prowess, and then slung the pack on at the doorway.

"There are three creeks that feed into the Green between here and the Lake," said the old man. "Choose the third one you come across."

"Yes sir. Thank you, sir."

"All right, then."

He closed the door sharply behind me once I was on the patio in the baking hot sun. The pack felt strange in its new weight. There was more in it, but it felt lighter.

I trekked back to the river, looking back every so often just to make sure, out of that slim remainder of suspicion, that the old man wasn't leveling a sniper rifle at my head for the kill shot. But he wasn't. There was just the trailer house humming with air conditioning, and a wooden canoe, freshly waxed, leaning against the wall in the shade.

I stopped at the river and stripped and swam in a pool at the foot of a small waterfall. It felt good, and I needed it. Then I sat naked on one of the rocks, drying within ten minutes. After putting on my clothes I stared downstream again, along this river pointing to Texas, pointing to Jordan. The abandoned brothel peeked over the branches. And it was like I was closing the door on an old haunt. I said, "Okay," and then headed towards Camp Woodward. Away from everything else.

June 25th

It's a narrow path to get back home. People wonder why there can't be many roads to truth. Why every highway but one has to be a dead end. Say, though, that there really *is* only one destination.

Here at Camp Woodward and barely in one piece.

This morning, Jenni walked into the nurse's station, where I finally managed to sit up and rest my elbows on a sterile folding table, and sat down across from me in a cold metal chair. A lone wasp sought escape in the corner of the window. Sunshine glared through the pane and ignited her joined hands. I didn't say anything to her. Just stared at the table. I'm told Carey and Jared were here last night. I'm also told Mom and Dad flew home from New York early to help the search team. That might be worth noting. Carey called the cops and they had search teams out around town, although none of them ventured very far up the river. Fortunate for Jordan, probably—they might have chanced upon the original fugitive in their attempts to recover *me*.

The last thing I remember is the pool where the creek met the Green River. It was the third one, like the old man said, and I waded across the Green, and was about to come up out on dry land when the water moccasin darted off a throne of a log in the shallows and nabbed me in the thigh. Surprise must've been what bowled me over. I hit my head on a rock sticking out of the bank. The snake bit me a couple more times at least, but my head was its own problem. I bled from the temple.

I must've been able to flop ashore, because a minute more of that and I would have been floating face down, bloated, and dead in the water.

Now Jenni and I sat across from each other. She was bright eyed and vivacious per usual. But she was on the verge of tears. It has been quite the summer for her, you know. Parents wanting answers. Demanding her to be fired for hiring a kid like Jordan. And now one of her veteran fellows goes missing for two weeks and comes up snake-bitten and concussed?

"How're you feeling?" she asked.

"Pretty sore. But I'm all right."

"You missed a few days of camp."

"Sorry about that."

"You're forgiven."

"How have things been here?" It was comical, this evasion of the catastrophe at hand.

"Oh you know! Between the new round of cop cars, your worried-to-death family, and even a journalist from *The Oklahoman* wondering if there was a reason for the 'spate'—she used that word, by the way—of disappearances of staff members here at Camp Woodward, I'd say things are pretty dang close to normal."

I shivered, sensing an impending headache that was probably caused by a mixture of dehydration, coffee withdrawal, and spiritual anxiety.

"I'm sorry, Jenni." I raised my head, leaning it backwards a little bit to achieve the appearance of aloofness and slight dissipation, and said, "I hope you're mad at me."

She frowned, cocking her head and going, "What?"

"I said I hope you're mad at me. Furious."

"I am furious. At a lot of things. You're not quite on the list."

"Wish I could be afforded the honor."

"You want me to be angry at you for getting yourself mixed up in the woods, looking for Jordan. At least, that's what I assume you were up to."

"Yes ma'am. It's no secret."

"I'm not mad at you for doing it. Why would I be?"

"I don't know." I felt myself starting to tear up, and brought my hand up to wipe the stupid tears away. "I don't know why anyone would think of me. Let alone be mad at me."

If ever there was a warrior against my unabating self-pity, it was Jenni. But she didn't flare up against it. She only remained calmly poised, scooting a cup of coffee toward me, and watched me cry. It was the strangest thing. Weeping freely in front of her. The depth of my shame out on the folding table, making the coffee tremor. Not knowing why I was feeling ashamed. The wasp, meanwhile, managed its escape through a crack in the caulk, and its buzzing mania was replaced by the laughter of some kids who ran by the heavy metal door on their way to the waterfront. I wasn't crying about Jordan anymore. I don't know what I was crying about. I never cry. Never. Least of all never in *front* of anybody.

"You know what I'm mad at?" she whispered. She couldn't have gotten a reply at that moment in time, so she went on, "I'm mad at all the lies you were told. It's hard, because you think you've been told the whole truth and nothing but the truth your whole life. But just because we're at a so called religious camp doesn't mean we're automatic saints. Or that we're immune from sin. It's in your name, Hunter *Saint*. You're not supposed to be a sinner. Or so you've been told."

"I *am* a sinner," I cooed. "The biggest sinner on the planet."

"You think that's humility. I can see that you do. That you're fallen too short, that you have to prove something."

"I wanted to find him."

"I know you did."

"I wanted to *help* him."

"I know you did."

"There's a lot of things I could've done and never did. I think of all the people I could've talked to who looked lonely, or freakish, or outcast, and I never did. Never."

"You talked to him. Don't you remember? You talked to him. You've helped a lot of people."

"Barely. But I didn't want to. I didn't like the kid. You want to know the truth, Jenni? I was *scared* of him. I didn't understand him, so I was *scared* of him. That's what kills me. He's just a little bit different and I treat him like a freak. Like he's someone who needs rehabilitation if only he can make someone like *me* comfortable. It's all a joke. Just a big, stupid joke."

"All right. It's okay. It's okay. Your family is still here, you know. You want to see them?" She put her hand on my forearm, which with the help of its counterpart buttressed my sobbing head. All that time of apparent soul searching in the wilderness and for what? I guess just a nervous breakdown.

"Oh God," I said. "I can't do it."

"They're not mad at you," Jenni said. "Honey. They're not mad you. No one's mad at you for trying to find that kid."

I stabilized a little bit, mopping my face dry and leaning back against the wall. It occurred to me then to attend to the elephant in the room, who was swishing its sheepish trunk to and fro by the door. In a raw voice, I asked, "Who found me out there, Jenni?"

Jenni sighed. "Who? Do you even know?"

"None of us is sure," she said. "Jerry and Lorrie found you on the dock, unconscious."

"The dock? There's no way. I got bit about a mile out from camp. It might even have been *more* than a mile."

"They said they didn't see anyone, but it was dark, and maybe they saw the wake of a boat."

I thought of the old man in the woods. Who else could it have been?

"Okay," I said. "Weird. I think I would have died if they hadn't found me. You know?" Jenni nodded. "Yeah," she said.

"I can go out to see my family."

"They're in the caf."

I limped from the nurse's station to the cafeteria with Jenni prefacing the journey in front of me and was met with the simultaneous cries of my mother and sister and the joint murmurs of relief from Jared and Dad.

It was only when their storm of affection ceased and I made it back to the bunk in the nurse's station before lunch with the rest of the staff that I opened up this half-waterlogged sketchbook of a journal and opened it to the first blank page, where I read in a script that looked vaguely familiar:

I hope you're okay, Hunter.

I dug through the rest of the pack. The pistol was gone.

June 26th

Breakfast this morning: lots of concern and timid questions. Lots of cautious side hugs. The present camp was told of my near-death-experience and so now its fleet of youth pastors are coming up to express their heartfelt concern for my recovery. Zach and I hugged the hardest. Lorrie, though, has only been watching me from a distance constructed of mutually established sadness.

I'm not well enough to get back in the swing of things, but neither do I earn the sole right to the nurse's station anymore. So, I've been in the Snack Shack, tendering orders for chicken strips and Dr. Peppers, and pouring rations of pickle juice into plastic containers.

No letter came from either OU or Johns Hopkins during my absence. It's weird. I didn't think about any of that stuff out in the woods, and don't really care about it now.

Dinner tonight: a big camp, all said and done. Jenni is her usual self, though at dinners, when it's busiest, she stands by the kitchen door with her hands behind her back, bobbing back and forth and chewing her lip.

June 27th

Mom and Dad came up again today to check up on me around lunchtime. Carey and Jared have been moving into their new place in the meanwhile, but said they'd visit over the weekend after they had settled in. Carey texted me (a rare phenom) to let me know that when my butt was safe and sound she had absolute permission to lay into me for being a stupid moron and leaving the way I did. Knew I could count on her at least for the fury I deserved.

Mom asked if it hurt much, and I said no, not really anymore. Touching the bite still stung a bit, but the camp life was starting to run on its old tracks. Sure, everyone was shook. I didn't think many people thought much of me at camp aside from Jenni, Lorrie, and Zach, but apparently, they started prayer groups for me while I was in the woods, and everyone was in on them. It makes you feel kind of guilty, in a different way.

Dad asked me if I'd heard from Johns Hopkins or OU, and I said no. He said, "Oh, yeah, well, you will. You will."

They drove off right before dinner time began.

Zach and I ate together before all the kids got to the caf. It was sloppy joe night. He observed the pocks on my bare arms as he chewed, and then asked if I'd spoken to Lorrie yet.

"About what?" I asked.

"I don't know. Just in general."

"I haven't. I don't know what to say, honestly."

Lorrie came in the caf between Jenni and Gabbie Reese, and put her backpack in the back closet where we keep all the chairs. She reemerged on the stage, adjusting her ponytail and scratching that itch she always seems to have on her upper shoulder.

"Do you still like her?" Zach asked.

I swallowed a mouthful of cowboy beans, and said, "Yeah. I do."

Zach gestured at me with his spoon, eyeing me down its silver rod. "She was a wreck when you were gone."

"A wreck."

"Yeah, buddy. I've never seen her like that."

"Define, wreck, will you?"

"Sure. Wreck: meaning utter devastated condition, non-functioning and generally inept at tasks formerly able to be rendered in full confidence."

"You been reading a dictionary during your quiet times?"

"As a matter of fact, I have been reading more!"

Lorrie was at the food line.

"I'm just saying, man, people here really came together for you. They even started a Facebook page, and in three days it had 1,000 members. Isn't that something?"

I hadn't known that. It sort of stopped me cold in mid-chew. "1,000 people were on the page?" I don't really check Facebook anymore, so it had totally escaped my notice.

"Yeah man. I think even one of our state representatives Tweeted about it."

"What?"

"Yeah, I know." Zach sighed and rubbed his calloused hands together, looking askance under his tight set flat bill hat. He blinked heavily. His dang knee was vibrating under the table.

"You all right, bro?"

"Thought you were dead, man," he said, ducking so I couldn't see his face. "All of us thought you were dead out there at one point. Didn't you think about that? Did you have to be so selfish?"

I set down my spoon. Lorrie sat down on the other side of the cafeteria and joined her hands and bowed her head in her customary prayer.

"I'm sorry, man. I don't know what came over me a couple weeks ago. It was just—you know, we were supposed to befriend that kid. It wasn't anybody's fault. I wasn't doing anything at home except sitting around feeling like crap about the whole thing. So I went out."

"I started looking for you, too."

"You did?"

"Of course! You think I was just gonna sit on my butt up and here and not look for you?"

"You didn't know where to look."

"Neither did you. You have no idea where Jordan is."

"I met someone in the woods who gave him food."

"The guy who hauled you in?"

"It would have to be. I don't remember, though."

Zach nodded, showing his face and the red tearfulness around his traditionally Stoic eyes. "Thank God he did find you. I've heard horror stories about water moccasin bites. Those are some tough buggers."

"It was a miracle. Probably."

"Yeah. All right. I'm in the dish room tonight. But come swimming afterward."

I helped sweep the cafeteria as the evening freneticism waned and the kids filed outside to go to the evening worship service.

Some of the staffers trekked down to the dock to swim across the lake, Lorrie among them, but I trailed off in the opposite direction and found myself in the cold back foyer of the worship center. The band was already sashed in fog and lolling lights, as if they were Radiohead or something such, with all the middle school aged kiddos piling in with their youth pastors, team leaders, and other spiritual coordinators. There weren't any chairs where I was standing, and part of the stage was obscured by the media roost where they work the slides and audio and all that.

The more the crowd grew and the louder the music swelled, and the longer people streamed by me without a second glance, the more solitary and out of place I felt. 1,000 people were praying for me when I was hiking out in the woods. I was gone for a week and a half. I got a statewide prayer initiative, and Jordan got a police report.

By the time the music actually started and the dark crowd swayed and jittered at the smoky altar, I had a frog in my throat the dimensions of a baseball and the impending sense that absolutely everything in the universe had been established the wrong side up.

I had to leave before the sermon even started and went up to my bunk in the dorms to recuperate and write. No one else is here right now. All of Jordan's stuff is gone. His bunk is skeletal and the wall behind it dull gray, signifying nothing, signifying mystery.

What *if*? Seriously, God—I wish you'd give me a hunch. What if my rescuer on the Green River was the pagan himself?

June 28th

Went back to lifeguarding at long last. It was in the upper nineties today, so the kids were at the waterfront in swarms. It's always somewhat of a miracle that a kid doesn't die weekly at these camps. The waterfront is so muddy, and when there are dozens of tiny children flopping around in the shallow end, risking concussion at every dunk, it's no small wonder that a few of them don't slip under unnoticed. Our lifeguards are good at what they do, though. We go through the proper training every summer. Everyone keeps a vigilant eye out. I admit, though, that today I kept scouring the lake beyond the waterfront to see any hints of a canoe on the far shores. Of course, there was nothing out there except the jet ski whirling around in circles.

No clouds in sight, today.

I need to talk to Lorrie.

Every day it gets easier to avoid her and but more burdensome on me not to.

What do we owe each other? It's not like we're dating. Perhaps on a vague trajectory toward courtship, but that's every summer. Who am I kidding, I mean, really?

I probably need to look at my cell phone, too. It's lying dead on the nightstand, but my time in the woods has sort of broken me of the habit, as well as the underlying need to look at it. Camp cures me of the tech addiction, usually, and redeems my attention span. But I always go back to it sooner or later. It's a necessary evil these days, they say. Carey and Jared must've brought the phone back when they drove up to camp. I don't know. I don't want to be bombarded by all the texts and calls that came in while I was out in the woods. Being away from it for this long has disbanded the illusion that I need it to stay connected to other people.

Is there something Jenni isn't telling me?

June 29th

Another camp gone, another free day before the next iteration of chaos.

Jenni still has me on a light diet and so commanded I ironically clean the nurse's station and no more, which I managed in under an hour, and thereafter wandered the perimeters of camp searching for trash. It's not actually often a staffer gets the chance to walk around the premises. So I did. I visited the basketball court, still littered with mangy basketballs unfit for play. These I picked up and deposited back in their crate, and then picked up the little bouquets of cone paper cups from underneath the water jugs.

As I walked across the open field on my way to the rock wall, which is the singular edifice in the opening aside from the octagonal gaga ball courts, Lorrie appeared. She was hauling a tub of climbing harnesses out of a compartment in the rock wall, which she slipped back into without seeing me.

She was judgment and pathos incarnate, turning me on my heels and sending me westward back to the cafeteria like a hot wind. I'd go trash sweep down the hill, evade notice, and arrange a meeting with her later. That's denial. The only way we'll ever speak again is via divine interception.

I stuffed sandy socks and coke cans into my trash bag in front of the party barn, wondering if it wasn't wiser to seek refuge in one of the dorms where Zach and the twins were mopping, sweeping, and de-pooping the bathroom stalls. Carli emerged from the Snack Shack to dump a fresh accumulation of mop water. She looked at me with the piercing intensity that only your almost-girlfriend's best friend is specialist in, as the water drained and seeped through the pebbles.

"Hey," I said.

"Trash sweeping already?"

"I had the nurse's station today."

"Huh." And then she was gone.

June 30th

Writing in the attic above the boy's dorm.

It made a lot of sense writing everything down out in the woods. At first, I thought I wouldn't do it, be it the lack of a proper desk or whatever, but out there the words were sort of my only companions. I had to write to stay sane, almost.

I checked my phone last night. Four hundred texts—some of them from strangers. I even glimpsed the Facebook page Zach mentioned. He wasn't kidding. It had 1,000 members strong, and they were still posting. Kathy Stone, a girl from my high school, shared a verse from Psalm 23 about how God leads his children from green pasture to green pasture, and how he had done that for Hunter Saint.

My aunt posted a picture, uncaptioned, of thick rays of light pouring through a formerly stormy ceiling of cumulous cloud. The word "hope" was engraved in papyrus style lettering across the sky.

There were twenty missed calls from Carey, all from that Sunday that I left. Then about fourteen from Mom and Dad combined, mostly delegated to the following Monday and Tuesday.

Lorrie seemed to have called once a day, in the evenings, with no voicemail, and no text messages. Once a day. No more, no less.

Jenni had texted, *Where are you???*

And from an unknown number: *You're a good man, Hunter. Stay safe.*

I called home, and Mom and Dad reported a mostly successful time in the Big Apple, save for the confusion at the subway station beneath Columbus Circle, the crowd outside the Broadway theater, and the incident in Central Park where Dad "accidentally" purchased rental bikes from a peddler.

Dad asked again about any letters of acceptance. No, not yet. He said it might be wise to look for alternatives. This stuff takes planning.

Mom said there's time for that. For now, I should rest a little bit, take it easy.

"I feel fine, Mom," I said.

"I looked up water moccasin bites," said Carey, who was still at home. "Buddy, you're a walking miracle. They're a type of pit viper."

"Oh!" Mom cried.

"Yeah. Honestly, whoever pulled you in probably sucked the venom from the bites to lessen the swelling and the effect long enough for you to get back to the nurse's station at camp."

"I don't doubt it," I said.

"Still no idea who it was, then, huh?" asked Jared

"No," I said. "At this point, my best guess is Jesus."

July 1st

It's the last adventure before the Fourth of July. This week's cohort is a small band of pollywogs from McKinney, TX. There are a mere hundred and twenty of them, which means quick meals, easy free time, and relaxed nights. A nightmare if you're trying to avoid contact with other non-busy staffers.

It's after dinner and I'm at the dock, pondering a swim across the lake. Zach said he'd come down later after taking a quick nap. He's been pretty tired lately. Not sleeping all that great.

Getting far into the second half of this journal and still a month left to go. Who would've thunk it? Maybe I chose the wrong profession! Writing is addicting, in a way. Making sense of the world, when you've been living more or less incognito for twenty some years, feels like taking oxygen. Catching up on years of unspent neglect. Thanks for that, Professor Snodgrass.

July 2nd

She came up on me so quietly last night that I didn't notice her until she sat down next to me. She didn't say a word. She wore her old gray running tank top but her hair was down. I glanced at her and put down the stupid sketchbook, no longer knowing what to do with my hands, my words, my life.

"I walked down here during the worship service we had after orientation," she said. "At the beginning of camp." Her voice was haggard, as if she'd just been to a Taylor Swift concert or had spent the preceding hours screaming over some injustice in the middle of the woods where no one would hear her. "I just needed some space, so I left. It was a sucky semester. The worst I've ever had."

"I'm sorry," I said. "I didn't know that."

"There was someone already here, though," she went on, unflinching. "And honestly, at first I thought it was you. You're always coming down here by yourself. But it wasn't you. It was Jordan."

My legs, although submerged in the lukewarm water, felt cold, and I don't know why but the tears jumped at my eyes.

"He was crying. Hard. I mean really, like, letting it all out. And he didn't hear me come up. I didn't want to bother him. I knew that if he saw me he would be embarrassed out of his mind. But I did think it was you, at first." She turned toward me for the first time that night, caramel brown eyes exploring me for a response, and went on, "I don't know if that means anything. I guess—don't hate yourself anymore. Please. It hurts me. God, it hurts me."

A smallmouth bass devoured a rehydrating mosquito a foot from our discourse and made a wake of dark water in its retreat.

I started to say something, but she cut me off, making the correct diagnosis and saying, "Don't say you're sorry. Please stop saying it. When you went missing for two weeks, yeah, I was mad. Worried sick, actually, and mad that I was worried sick, because that meant I actually cared about you, and more than as just a friend."

"Lorrie," I croaked, leaning forward in surrender. She put a finger to my nose, sabotaging the advance.

"Do you know who saved you?" she whispered.

I shook my head. "Do you?"

She bowed her head, kneading the back of her hand. "I don't know what all this means. That kid's never coming back. Maybe I shouldn't say."

I straightened up. "You saw?"

"Yeah. I was the one who heard the shouting and found you here."

"You and Jerry."

"We were filling up water jugs and were coming down to the water-front anyway."

"Who was it?"

She only took a deep breath of air but didn't reply.

"Lorrie, for God's sake."

She stood up all of a sudden, her bare feet half suspended over the water as if she was tempting her balance and clasped her hands to her cheeks.

"I can't be sure," she whispered. "The canoe was already almost around the corner. But I think it was him, Hunter. I've reimagined the scene a million times and I really think it was him."

"Then he's still close," I shouted, leaping to my feet. "He must have gone back for the canoe he lost and started coming back to camp." I hustled over to the canoe rack, intending on selecting the remaining good one, but Lorrie ran after me and grabbed my hand. "Please don't, Hunter." Now she was crying, pulling at me. "Let it go. Let it go. I failed him, too. We all did. Please."

The canoe was caught on one of the rack's suspension hooks. It hung upside down, trembling. It was more from my crazed impatience than the technical difficulties that made me try to rip the boat free, which told me that it was done performing the errands of stupid young men. I was, and am, at the end of my rope, though dangling as from my big toe, graced with an upside view of the universe.

July 4th

Gabe and Jerry did their firework show last night and the staff all laid on the hill overlooking the lake with hotdogs and watermelon slices. I sat next to Lorrie ripping grass up and swatting mosquitoes and peering off and on into the darkness to discern the meandering figures of the two men, one old and crab legged, the other tall and wiry, as they arranged their art on strips of plywood.

"Halfway done," said Lorrie, meaning the summer. Carli sat by her, chattering with excitement, and Jenni and Zach ambled up and sat behind us.

"Crazy," I said. She was right. It didn't feel like Independence Day. It still felt like May 24th on the first day of camp and that all we've had so far are false starts. Camp hasn't really started yet. It can't really be halfway over. That's a nutso thing to claim. I kept watching Jerry bend down with his head craned upward to observe and imitate Gabe, as if there was something holy and implacable in the old man's method of putting artillery shells in a row. I kept thinking about how I told Jordan where Jerry's gun was, and how he still doesn't know, and that no one knows, and probably never will. Nobody knows it was my fault.

July 5th

Swam across the lake last night. I haven't done it since May, before the debacle and whatnot, and didn't realize how out of shape I was. When I was halfway across the lake on my way back, someone stood on the dock with hands in pockets, staring at me. I went underwater and blew the air through my nose and dared to open my eyes for a second just to see the blurry blades of sun shudder through the murk. When I came up and wiped my hair out of my eyes, the figure on the dock was gone and I wasn't even sure I'd seen anybody there to begin with.

Is this what it feels like when a soldier gets back from war? I don't want to be trite with comparisons, but being out in the woods for two weeks, getting bit by a snake, and then having someone haul me into safety and in effect saving my life did contain the aura of battle. On the dock, I checked the scar on my thigh. Small red-yellow scars no bigger than pin pricks. Is this what that feels like? Can you really live in this world if you haven't come at least somewhat close to dying? Maybe that's what happened to Jordan in the rec field. He realized that he could end his own life, that the idea was no longer theoretical but armed with bullets, and how that kind of power isn't to be lightly tampered with. Once he felt the barrel resting under his chin, he saw the world for what it was: an astonishingly extravagant gift. Problem was, he had already given it away.

July 6th,

One time when we were kids, Mom and Dad took us all to a national park in Colorado. We camped by this river running swiftly with snowmelt from the mountains. A pine tree had fallen over the river a few yards downstream, and I remember making a game out of balancing on it and crossing to the other side when no one else was around. Sometimes I paused right in the middle of the log with my arms spread to either side, training my eyes on the white tongues of current rushing beneath me. The roar of the water and the blunt freshness of the pines and the idea of being swept into the river's power was all right there, fomenting mercilessly before my feet.

I fell in. After a while my boots got slippery and I toppled into the current like a sardine. The river thrust me through two boulders and then carried me into an eddy twenty yards down, where I thrashed and gurgled and then got folded back into the current and rolled down the rapids with about the power of a kitten in a blender. Then I was spat Jonah-style on a bank of pebbles and lay there with my legs still sucked by current, but I grabbed the root of a nearby shrub and managed to drag myself all the way ashore. I threw up water and lay on my back, wondering how far I had floated, until finally I stood up and realized my boots and socks were gone. But it didn't matter. I could've been naked for all I cared.

July 7th

Today: lifeguarding from 1-4, dinner at 5, Snack Shack duty from 7-9. Have two hours in the morning free. Need to check email for updates on med school. Lorrie and I have been taking walks during our free time. We are officially attracting grins and glances. When two Baptists start dating, it's like a meteorite has smashed into planet Singleness and every other solar system within proper range has witnessed the awesome doom and can't stop sending flares. But we haven't decided yet. Mainly we've just been talking about our lives and we've been talking about the past, which we both only recently realized we had never talked about before, and which further indicates that we didn't really know each other whatsoever before this crazy summer.

July 9th

A carnival came through Adler yesterday and some of us from camp went, since it was a free day—me, Zach, Lorrie, and Carli. The janky rides glimmered even from a distance, shrouded in upset dust from hundreds of the entertained. It cost ten bucks to get in. The great tomahawk ride, which graces our lowly village every summer, shingled with yellow bulbs, swung upside down and stayed suspended for five seconds with the women's hair hanging down and a couple of children screaming for escape, and then it swung down toward the earth as we watched with our funnel cakes in hand. It's a miracle it never breaks. It was a hammer sent to judge the earth or scrape it just to show the gash it could make. A politically incorrect chieftain grinned on its rusty side. The tomahawk eased to a stop, back and forth and back and then still, and the thin men with leather and tattoos for skin swung open the gate and let the riders dribble out in a woozy file.

"Want to do it?" said Zach.

A flock of middle schoolers in tank tops and crocs rushed in line in front of us. "Keep your paws *off* the fence!" one of the workers barked.

"I don't know," I said. "Not really, honestly."

"Aw c'mon, let's do it!" said Carli.

"I do NOT trust that thing," said Lorrie, bunching up her brows.

Zach and Carli glanced at each other. Lorrie and I glanced at each other. We all know how it goes. Carli just broke up via phone with her boyfriend, Tyler, who I actually know pretty well, and Zach has not so subtly been making advances.

I told them to go for it, but that we'd do it the next time. Maybe. They cast wry glances at each other and back at us as they joined ranks with the junior high kids and were shown to the flaky leather seats with seatbelts that weren't much more than paracord strips that might have been swiped from a military convention.

We watched them get strapped in, feet dangling, with Zach grinning and Carli starting to go, "Let me off, let me off, let me off." But there was no getting off now and the tomahawk lurched backwards, preparing to swing.

"You having any fun at all?" I asked Lorrie.

"Yeah, of course!" She studied me with open eyes, searchingly. Her eyes flashed in the evening sunshine, runed with helixes of dust. The air smelled of dirty people, cattle manure, and straw.

"Are you?" she asked.

I smiled, shrugged. "Yeah. It's the same every year, you know." I asked her if she wanted a candy apple. She likes those. She said no, and we watched the tomahawk crank back to a ninety-degree angle, pause in midair for a few seconds, and then careen forth to manage its first radial ascent.

"Do you actually want to do it next?" Lorrie said.

"I really don't," I said, and laughed. "I did it last year. But I don't know. Not really feeling it tonight."

"Me neither."

As our friends shook hands with death on the racist roller coaster, Lorrie and I walked around the carnival. We passed by some kind of game where you throw hoops and try to catch them on nails sticking out of a piece of plywood. Then we passed the carousel and its royal little horses undulating to bad organ music with children and their fathers atop them. Some of the kids had troubled expressions that seemed to say, "Is this it?"

We stopped to look at that year's crop of bunny rabbits. A gray, lop-eared fellow observed us with its liquid black eyes, breathing so fast I wondered if it was on the cusp of a stroke. It sucked water from its tube in the corner of the cage and faced us again with its nostrils blinking. It kicked up some mulch with a hind leg and bid us goodbye by peeing.

Finally, I saw a little boy standing alone and pointing at a massive stuffed bear hanging on the door of a basketball popup. He must have thought someone was next to him because he was saying, "Daddy, look at *that*!" But he was all by himself. He ran up to the stand and tried to touch the bear's foot, the only part of it in reach, but the teenager punk behind the counter shooed him away. "That's not yours!" The boy realized he was alone, then, and spun around every which way, then started to scream, "Daddy! Daddy!" until Lorrie and I almost came to help him. But a young man, pale-faced and out of breath, swooped him up from behind and held him for a few seconds as he cried, and the boy no longer seemed interested in the toy.

When we got back to camp, it was still light out, so I walked down to the dock by myself for a swim. Lorrie and I didn't ride the tomahawk, and both Zach and Carli ended up sort of sick and wishing they hadn't indulged. We all felt a little sick from the funnel cakes. I also got a luke-warm corndog for whatever reason, if only because county fairs demand you shorten your lifespan by at least five years. A night by the water might heal both body and soul.

The trees on the far side of the lake were reflected on the water's rim. The light of Gabe's house made a white satellite among the branches. A lonely, artificial sun. I dove off the dock, curling up underwater for a few seconds, and then climbed back up. It was a clear evening. The sky itself was like a body of water. I thought of the tomahawk, and what kind of view Zach and Carli had of the world when they were upside down in that motionless apex. So, I planted my hands on the dock, spread my knees and notched them above my elbows, and then slowly eased my head down and my legs upward until my head rested on the dock and I had the reordered perspective I wanted. Trembling and with a blood-filled face, the reflections of the trees became the trees, and the lake became the sky, and the sky became the lake, and the ripples of the lake became signals from a distant planet, trying to communicate something. Maybe if I stayed upside down for long enough, I'd know what the signals were saying.

I lost my balance after ten seconds and toppled back into the water, grappling the edge of the dock for support, and when I looked up, Lorrie stood there, wanting to talk.

July 10th

"It's been a weird summer."

"You're telling me."

"I get that it was weird because of all the Jordan stuff, and then it just got insane when you disappeared for two weeks in the woods. I don't think I have ever been that scared."

"I'm sorry."

"We've been through that. You don't have to apologize."

"I think I do. I left without telling anybody and justified it by having this weird sense of being a martyr or something, like this was my punishment for not taking Jordan under my wing like Jenni asked."

"She asked all of the veterans to take him under our wing. Me, Zach, Carli. Jerry."

"Yeah. I know. I know."

"Anyway. What I was going to say is that it was weird before the summer. Coming into Camp Woodward, I mean."

"Because you had a bad semester, or something?"

"Sort of. I never really told you exactly what was going on."

"You don't have to if you don't want to."

"No, I want to. It felt so weird coming back to camp because I wasn't sure I believed in God anymore."

"Oh."

"Yeah."

"Well. Okay."

"It had sort of been growing for a few months. Maybe even years. All my professors are pretty vocal against invoking God as a way to explain the world. For them it's unscientific. It can all be explained materially if only you give it the light of the day."

"Right."

"But I don't know—over time it just got to wearing down on me, and I didn't have many Christian friends, and I realized that no one had ever told me about why we believe what we do. I mean, I had questions in high school. I wanted to know how evolution and God might both be real at the same time. Or why God allowed so much suffering in the world if he was all good. Your basic stuff that people naturally wonder about. But no one really talked about that in our church."

"No, you're right. I can't remember being given many answers either, or reasons why Christianity might actually be *true*. I guess it was just what we grew up with."

"It was all we really knew. And that's fine, but I just started meeting all these people at school who seemed really nice and happy and normal and who didn't see much of a need to, like, believe in God or to repent of their sins or anything. I met this Buddhist girl, and she seemed like such a deep and kind soul. More spiritually disciplined than *I've* ever been. So by spring break I was seriously questioning everything. Absolutely everything. And I didn't know who to talk to about it because I wasn't sure if my dad would understand. And I didn't want my mom to freak out. You know how she gets. Telling her I was losing my faith would probably give her a heart attack."

"I get that."

"So, I didn't talk to anybody about it. I started reading different religious texts in the library, like the Bhagavad Gita and the Quran, quotes from Siddhartha. I read Sanskrit literature and Native American thought. I read Charles Darwin's stuff and some of the philosophers from the Enlightenment. And then one day I was sitting in the foyer of the library and suddenly realized I didn't believe in God anymore. Or at least, not the version of God I was taught about."

"Man. I don't really know what to say."

"That's not quite the end of the story. At first it felt sort of like a relief. That I was finally 'free,' whatever that means. I did some crazy stuff the next couple weeks."

"You don't have to go into detail."

"Ha, thanks. Yeah, you don't want to know. And I don't want to remember. By then, it was April and Jenni had sent me my returning staffer email and all I had to do was electronically sign it and send it back. I guess if anyone would understand my situation it would be Jenni. I mean, I didn't want to come here to a conservative Christian camp that takes pride in saving souls for Christ and pretend that I was on board with it. It made me feel sick, the pretending. And I didn't want to be left out at the same time. I was about to call her and back out and spill the beans, but I didn't, and I signed it and I sent it to her and Carli and I drove out here same as we've always done, summer after summer."

"So you were still doubting really hard when we got here in May."

"Yeah. I'd say it got even worse here. I felt like such a fake. Like if anybody knew what I was going through they would reject me, and I didn't want that. It's one of those things you don't really tell people who have looked up to you as such an example of the faith, or as someone who treats faith as the most important thing in the world. I just couldn't do it. So I faked it. I went to the Bible studies and prayed over meals. I gave my devotional and testimony to the staff that morning in June and carried my Bible in my backpack like I always used to. The problem is I didn't know what I believed. I guess you could say 'science,' but that doesn't really mean anything. Science is something people *do*, it's not a belief system, and the science is always changing. Always. What Darwin thought about the cell has been debunked by a microscope. And you know all about quantum mechanics, how that threw everything for a loop."

"Yeah."

"So I didn't know what to believe. It was a weird where I was skeptical of everything, including my own skepticism. It got to the point where I saw a bird in a tree and wondered in what sense it was really *there* at all."

"Dang. You weren't kidding around."

"I mean, what is consciousness, even? I don't mean to sound dramatic, but if we're just assemblies of neurons and meat then at best it's an illusion. The bird in the tree, and the tree, not to mention religion, is a figment of our imaginations. So why bother about whether God is real or not? It doesn't matter if you believe it or not. But these science guys are just as evangelistic in their conversion efforts as Pastor Bill. They want to persuade you to a version of reality. They're just as religious as we are at Camp Woodward."

"That's pretty insightful. I hadn't really thought of it like that before."

"So I was going kind of nuts. And then Jordan shot the gun and ran away, and then a few days later *you* ran away, and I realized, 'Shoot, I want to be with Hunter and I never truly realized it until now. He's a good man. He's looking after that kid because he actually cares. That means he'll care for me, too. If he can care about someone that gnarly and pagan, then he can listen to me, too. Only I don't think I can be with him if I'm not a Christian.'"

"That would put a wrench in things, probably. I don't know. Where are you at now with all this?"

"It's weird. Every night I started going down to the dock, right here, and looked for you. I even took one of the canoes out and went all the way down one of the channels. Zach came with me a couple of times."

"He mentioned that. You didn't have to do that for me."

"Well. I wanted to. But one night, I was sitting here and looking at the stars, and I thought about what you said a few months ago. About your experience with God by the water jug in the rec field. I felt panicked. Like, if there's really no God then no one is there to witness me here in this moment. And that means no one, not even people who love you, can really witness you either. It's matter and energy all the way down. No information. No communication. No Mind. The thought terrified me. I don't think people really come to grips with their propositions when they say we're nothing but meat but that we should for some reason be good and virtuous people anyway. But I just had this thought that if God didn't really exist then I was, like, completely alone in the universe. There's no other way around it. They beat God out of me but God came back. What did they call him in olden days? The necessary Being?"

"Something like that."

"And then, right when I had that moment, I prayed for you out loud, just asking that God would bring you back. Later that night you showed up. Unconscious, but in one piece."

"An answer to prayer?"

"I don't know. Probably. Or just a wonderful coincidence. I went to the worship sanctuary that night and just cried, Hunter. Thanking God for you. For everything. I'm still struggling, and I still have questions, but…it's going somewhere, now, I think."

"You're not alone. You were never alone in that. We've all had doubts. I'd be more worried about the person who *doesn't* have doubts. You know? I get how you feel to an extent. I think this whole summer has made me realize how little I've questioned things I believe. Not that I want to be cynical. I've been thinking a lot about dying, though, probably since I was *this* close to dying just two weeks ago. It's like coming up out of the water after being held under for four minutes. Everything pops. I mean, I could roll around in the mud right now. I just want to be honest. I think you do, too."

"I like you a lot."

"I like you, too."

"That's me being honest."

"Okay."

"I think God is maybe real and that He saved you."

"You do?"

"Yeah. I do."

"I think Jordan saved me. You said so yourself."

"They can both be true."

July 15th

This afternoon, I was in the Snack Shack with Zach and Jenni, and a few elementary age kids were sucking popsicles and pickle pops at the tables.

Jenni got a call and took it to the kitchen, and then came out a couple minutes later and took me back to the kitchen, too.

"*The Oklahoman* wants to send a reporter to Camp Woodward," she said. "Again. Only this time they want to interview *you*."

"Me? What for?"

"I guess they want to talk to you about your being out in the woods looking for Jordan for two weeks." Jenni bit her lip. "You don't have to do this. They asked if it was okay, but I said I'd ask you first and then let them know."

"I mean, I don't know, I guess it's fine," I said. "Are they doing some longform essay about him or something?"

"I don't know."

"And they're coming all the way out here."

"Yep. Apparently the reporter wants to take a tour around the camp and get a feel for the place. That's what she said on the phone."

"Ah, it's a *woman*!"

Jenni sighed, and then leaned her head back and went, "Ugggh—uh!" and laid her head down on the metal chopping table in front of the pizza ovens.

"What's the matter?"

"I don't know," she said, muffled. "What do people think of us, Hunter?"

"Like, what do they think of Camp Woodward?"

"Yeah. What do they think of Camp Woodward?"

"I don't know, honestly. I mean, not many people have heard of us."

"That's not it." She settled her head in her hands and bounced the end of her shoe against the floor. "I started managing the camp four years ago. Your first summer working here." She does this thing where she'll grip the far edge of the surface she's leaning against and crouch down so her chin is resting on the edge, like she's preparing for a distant atomic blast. "I always thought we might get into the news someday for a revival that broke out. I didn't really care about Camp Woodward getting clout, but if we were gonna be known for anything, I wanted it to be positive. Who wouldn't?" She straightened out and put her face back into her hands again. "Now we're known for a teenager staffer who almost shot a bunch of children in our rec field. How did he even know where that gun was? I can't help but think that the caption for an article like this might read something like—" She straightened and pinched her index and thumb close together and set imaginary type in the air— "'shooting incident reveals the dysfunction and hidden darkness of youth church culture.'" She threw her hands up and said, "I can't control the narrative. But no one's going to want to come here anymore when they read something like *that*." I've never seen Jenni cry or get panicked, but she started to breathe deeply through her nostrils while her lips tightened and she clenched and unclenched her jaw, hands on her hips.

Everything is still so fresh when I think about it. Maybe it felt like a lifetime for me since I almost died in the woods and then came out on the other side, but it has only been a month since Jordan shot the gun and took off. It has only been a couple of weeks since I mysteriously floated back into the premises.

"Tell the reporter to come," I said. "I'll talk to her. I'll tell her what happened. You can, too. I feel like everyone who actually walks around Camp Woodward and meets you has a positive impression. It's a good place. It's helped a lot of people."

"Yeah. I know. I just—I feel like I did something to deserve this and I can't figure out what."

What was I going to tell this reporter? What was she going to *ask*? Was she going to pry about Camp Woodward's management? No. She was going to ask about Jordan. How well I knew him. What our relationship was like. Why I went after him.

How he got that gun.

"I'll set the record straight, if she asks a bunch of dumb questions," I said. "Don't worry. I think we're overthinking this, Jenni."

Jenni didn't reply. She took her phone out and called *The Oklahoman* and said okay, we'd be willing to talk, and I heard a woman's chipper voice reply, "Great! I'll try and get there around 4 p.m. if that works."

She hung up and looked at me and we both took a big breath and widened our eyes. "Just tell the truth," she said, and shrugged. "Then you don't have to remember what you said."

I worked at the Snack Shack until 3:30 and then went up to my bed in the dorms where I laid in the empty darkness for twenty minutes. Zach came in and laid down in his bunk, exhaling and going, "So you're talking with the reporter?"

"I guess so, man."

"Exciting." There was artificiality in his voice. Distance. I heard him roll on his side and a couple minutes later he was snoring.

The reporter came at 4 p.m. as promised, driving a sleek Honda civic newly browned from the dust of unfamiliar country roads. I got to Jenni's office and we both looked down on her as she crunched over the pebbles and parked in front of the building. "She doesn't even have *The Oklahoman* logo stamped on the side!" I said.

"How do we know who she really is?"

"She could be anybody."

"She could be from *The New York Times*."

"Yikes."

"She could be a spy."

"Even better."

"Spying out rural America to glean all our secrets."

"Not sure what secrets we have to hide, but yeah, yeah."

The reporter got out and perched a pair of aviators on top of her head, revealing her to be a blue-eyed blonde no older than twenty-five, dressed in a black cardigan and gray business pants. She had that furrowed brow look particular to journalists who are curious and skeptical of everything at the same time, and she glanced up at the window to see Jenni and me peering down upon her. She carried a composition notebook, spiral bound, with a large iPhone placed part and parcel on top of it.

"Shoot!" cried Jenni, retreating to her chair. "We've been spotted!" I sat at the table, no longer frivolous, feeling like I was about to be sat down by the FBI or the IRS or a miffed professor.

"What am I supposed to do? Just sit here?"

"I don't know," said Jenni. "I guess she'll want to talk to you privately or whatever."

"Well why doesn't she talk to both of us at the same time?"

"Maybe she will. I don't know!"

She knocked on the wall outside the open door and peeked her head inside—a blossom of frizzled blonde hair with electric blue eyes born to investigate the dark corners of the world. "Hello?" she said cheerily. Her lanyard dangled to her waist and I caught the name "Hannah."

"Hello! You must be from the paper," said Jenni, standing up and offering a handshake.

"Yes ma'am, that's me. Hannah Reardon. I'm an investigative reporter for *The Oklahoman*. Thank you so much for taking the time to talk with me."

"It's no problem."

Meanwhile I stood a couple yards behind Jenni trying to inconspicuously dry my sweating palms on my shorts. Hannah glanced behind Jenni's shoulder and nodded at me, going, "Are you…Hunter? Hunter Saint?"

I said that yes, I was Hunter Saint, and that I was "honored" to be able to talk to a real reporter, which then reddened me like a plum and had Hannah chuckling. She wasn't much older than me, shoot dang it.

"Well, I'd love to ask you some questions if that's all right. And maybe look around, too."

"Sure. Hunter can show you around. He knows the place as well as I do." I don't remember what I said in response to that, but it wasn't a poem to be recited, I know that much. Hannah gave another artificial laugh and then clicked her pen against the notepad and said, "All right! Where should we start?"

I took her outside first, in between the cafeteria and the party barn, where the camp was having a meeting before dinner about what they were doing that night.

"I guess there it doesn't matter too much where we start," I said. "I mean, is there anything in particular you wanted to see?"

She said she mainly wanted to get a sense of the camp itself. How big it was, how many buildings, what sort of people worked here. I said okay, and so we just started walking down the gravel loop. I pointed at the Snack Shack to our left. To the party barn, an open musty warehouse that's as wondrously dingy as it sounds. To the rock wall and Dorms 1, 2, 3, and 4. 800 max capacity, I said, when she asked how many kids could stay here at a time. "And that's how many kids were here when Jordan Caol shot the gun?"

"About that, yes."

We took the loop past Dorm 3 and arrived at the maintenance shed where the ground was still furrowed from its water pipe surgery. I hadn't been back here since we dug out the hole and Jerry lost his marbles over the missing gun. The night before Jordan shot the missing gun. The night he undoubtedly *stole* the missing gun.

I told her what happened with the water pipe, and when. She asked me nothing about the gun. I sensed that it was only a matter of time before she asked about it. Who wouldn't ask about it? That was kind of the big story here.

As we emerged next to Jerry's trailer house, I saw that she was recording me on her iPhone, and writing bullet points on the first page of the composition pad. Was this her first big story? She was young. I asked her where she went to college. "University of Oklahoma," she replied. "How about you?"

"Winston's College," I said. "Up in Illinois. You probably haven't heard of it."

"No, I have! Heard it's a good school."

"Yeah, I liked it." I was trying to keep up my enthusiasm, nodding a lot and smiling and crossing my arms to hide the sweat pools in my pits.

"So who lives there?" She pointed at Jerry's trailer house. I told her. She asked what Jerry did. I told her he worked maintenance. He replaced air conditioners and fixed water pipes. He killed all the snakes at the waterfront and scanned the edges of camp for coyotes.

"So he has guns?"

"A couple."

"Does he keep those locked up?"

"Well, he's got a conceal carry license, but I don't see him carry too often."

"Why does he have conceal carry license?" Her pen was poised against the paper.

"To protect the kids," I said. "And to kill armadillos and snakes."

We walked on. She stopped near the entry, where the green gate stood open and the gravel driveway roped down the hill. She observed it for a moment and asked if there was another entry. There wasn't.

"So what do you plan to do after this summer, Hunter?"

"The plan is to go to medical school starting hopefully in the spring."

"That's exciting."

"Yep. I applied to OU, actually."

"And where did you go to high school?"

"Adler High."

"How long have you worked at Camp Woodward? How many summers, I mean."

"Since the summer of 2014."

"So this is your...fourth year. Wow. A veteran."

"Yep."

"How have you liked working here?"

"It's a special place. I've always loved coming back. It's a lot of work but it's a ton of fun, too."

"Have you found, like, really good community here over the past four years?"

"Definitely. Jenni's a close friend, now. Zach, Lorrie, James and Rory. There's some new faces this year that I don't know as well, but it's pretty tightly knit."

"I noticed on the website that the staff size is small," said Hannah. "You don't hire over twenty people a summer?"

"Generally. It's small enough that we don't need more."

"But this year you had twelve."

"To begin with."

To think that I was the one who made the segway into the unruly terrain of Jordan was a prick of irony; Hannah ate it up.

"So tell me about your relationship with Jordan. If you're okay with that."

"There isn't too much to tell, unfortunately," I said. I sighed and resituated my ball cap on my head. My hair's getting way too long. "Jordan was a super quiet kid from the moment he got here. I tried to talk to him a couple of times, but he was pretty standoffish."

"Uh-huh. Did you ever have suspicions that he was planning something like this?"

"Oh, no. Not in a million years. You never think something like that will happen in a place like Camp Woodward."

"Do you know where he got the gun? Was it his?"

There we were on the cusp of the great question, with my own main question starting to burn within me now, accusing me of a major blunder: do I tell her that I told Jordan where the gun was? And why the crap didn't I talk to Jerry about it first? It was hard to imagine Jerry reading *The Oklahoman*, but he'd probably want to read *this* article. "Tell the truth," I heard Jenni saying somewhere in the subconscious realms. "Then you don't have to remember what you said."

"He stole it," I said. "He rummaged through one of our staffer's houses and found it."

"Oh, wow."

"Yeah."

"So it wasn't his."

"No. It wasn't his."

I bowed my head and wiped my brow and trained my eyes on the gravel ribbon we crunched upon with our slow, professional steps. I saw the canopy in the middle of the rec field and Jenni's little blue house and its chandelier of chimes swaying in the breeze.

"So why did you go after him, Hunter?" She had finished writing down a couple of full-length sentences that she must have thought needed to be recorded right then and there, and then scrutinized me again with those electric eyes. She had not, and never did, ask how Jordan knew where to find the pistol.

"I don't know," I said. A lie? Only halfway. "I mean, honestly it was a bit of a whim. I woke up Sunday morning after it happened, went to church with my sister and brother-in-law, and then before I even really knew what I was doing I had a bag packed and was out the door. It occurred to me that he might follow the Green River south from Camp Woodward, and so I might be able to catch him on his hike down. I was worried about him. We were off for two weeks because a couple of incoming camps had cancelled, and I just couldn't stop thinking about him."

"And you didn't run across him."

"Not exactly."

"What you mean?"

"I think we just barely missed each other. There's an old farmer who lives in a trailer house in the woods. He invited me over for lunch on the day before I made it back to camp, and he said Jordan had left just the day before."

"So Jordan had been staying with this old man in the woods."

"Apparently."

"And the police teams, the helicopters, the private investigators… none of them came across this old man in the woods?"

"I guess not. He was pretty well hidden."

"But *you* found him?"

"Not really. He found me. I was trespassing on *his* territory, technically."

"And you had lunch with him."

"Yes."

"And you talked about Jordan?"

"A little bit."

"What did he say, exactly?"

"Well, he said that Jordan had been here, all right, but that he'd left the morning day before. He said he was probably headed to Texas."

"Texas."

"That's right."

"What's in Texas?"

"His dad, apparently."

"So this kid was going to try and find his dad?"

A section of my innards jolted. She was no officer, but some basic record retrieval would quickly reveal the father's identity and maybe even have a reporter squad knocking on his door by the end of the week.

"That's what the old man suggested. But I don't know for sure. He never mentioned anything about his dad to me when he was a at camp."

"I see, I see."

We made it back to the cafeteria, and we stopped in to get out of the heat (99 degrees today and hotter tomorrow) and to have a glass of water and a cup of coffee. I got her the coffee from the eternal burner next to the kitchen and we sat down beneath the massive Big Ass fan. No one else was in there except for Margie the cook, who bustled in and out of the doorway with oven mitts and perturbation engraved on her face.

"Okay, so let me get this straight," said Hannah, sipping the coffee and joining her fingers together on the table. "Jordan gets hired here, stays here for less than two weeks. He steals a gun, fires it into the air, and then escapes via...was it a canoe?"

"Yep. He'd tangled the other canoes with a bunch of chains so we couldn't follow him."

"Wow. Okay. And that was it? He never showed his face again, no one heard from him whatsoever."

"So far as I know.

"Did his mom ever come to get his stuff?"

"I think so. I never met her, though."

"Huh."

"Yeah. It all happened pretty fast."

I told her about how it went in the woods. Putting up camp every night, sweating my pores out, crossing the river. I told her I had found the canoe Jordan had stolen from Camp Woodward, upturned in the river, and about the shoe findings, which Hannah recorded on her notepad with vigor. I told her about the abandoned brothel or whatever the heck that crumbling stone artifice used to be, recapped my time with the old man, whose name I had neglected to ask, but for the sake of the legend let's just call him "old man Kyle."

Then I told her all I could configure of my accident. The snake bite, the shock, the head hit on a rock, and the necessity of a savior to lug me back to Camp Woodward.

"Was it the old man?" said Hannah, pen suspended in her hand, wide-eyed. She was no longer a journalist but a child listening to a ghost story. *Tell the truth. Tell the truth…*

"I don't know," I said. "It could have been."

"Who *else* could it have been?"

"Well, I don't want to jump to any conclusions, but it could've been Jordan himself."

"You're kidding. What gives you that idea?"

"It's more of a feeling than an idea. It's possible that Jordan was in the old man's house the whole time I was there, hiding out in the back room in the trailer house. It's also possible that Jordan followed me as I started to make my way back to camp, and that he saw me get bit by the moccasin, hit my head in the shallows, and plucked me out before I drowned."

"But you said you arrived in a canoe, right?"

"Right. It's furthermore possible that Jordan ran back to the old man's house and got his wooden canoe, dragged it back, and floated me up the channel until we reached the lake. And then Lorrie and Jerry found me on the dock."

"That's your hypothesis. That the kid on the lam saved your life after you looked for him in the woods for two weeks."

"It's one of the possibilities. Who can tell for sure? It could've been the old man. I don't know. He was pretty old. I'm not sure he could've handled all the physical stress. But then again, Jordan's not a muscular kid. He probably weighs about 130 pounds all in all. It would've taken a ton of effort to pick me up, put me in a canoe, and paddle upstream a channel to reach the lake. I just take it on faith that somebody saved me because I know for a fact I conked out a mile away from Camp Woodward. You can look it up on a map. It's a mile exactly, where I got bit and hit my head."

"So this is a mystery."

"It sure is."

"But no sign of him since then? He hasn't come back at all?"

"Not that I know of. I don't know why he would."

"Sorry, I just have so many questions."

"So do I."

"Why do you think he shot the gun but didn't kill anyone?"

"I think he meant to kill someone," I said, now kneading my hands. "He positioned the gun under his chin before he chucked it. But he didn't do it."

"Any ideas why he did this? He didn't hurt anyone, from all accounts. He did it in a public place, and clearly posed a huge danger to those children, but he didn't do it."

"It's another doozy and I wish I had an answer for you."

It's weird being the guy who is supposed to know the story and can recount the story's details but nonetheless fails to elucidate motivations, meanings. Up to his point, she asked the "what" and the "how," but now trespassed into the grimy murk of the "why." The media already had the information, more or less. What no one had bothered to request until Hannah Reardon showed up was the purpose behind the information. The story in all this. Was there a story? She seemed to believe there was. She seemed to believe that the facts and the events were not random atoms bumping into each other but could *lead* somewhere if you just followed them far enough.

"You'd have to ask Jordan," I said. "Not for a minute do I want to defend him. What he did was terrible. He stole a dangerous weapon and he terrified 800 kids, and they're probably *still* terrified. He chose a coward's way to attract attention. But just being around him for a few days, I can say that we didn't treat him like we should. I know *I* didn't. I had sort of a saintly urge to take him under my wing, since I was older and have worked here so long, but when push came to shove I basically just left him alone and ignored him. He seemed to want to be left alone, but now I wonder if all he really needed was for someone to talk to him. Give him a chance to come out of the woodwork and help him wade through some things. I guess that's what every guy his age wants. A sense of direction. To be seen by a man who knows what the heck he's talking about. Only problem is that I don't think I know what I'm talking about."

"Yeah. That makes sense. Go on."

"He needed somebody to love him, basically. And I don't think any-body really did. Not to justify him stealing that gun, but that was his way of reminding everyone that he existed."

"Why do you think he didn't go through with the suicide?"

"It's another theory, but I've thought about it a lot. I think for the split second after he fired the gun he realized that he had absolutely zero interest in shooting anyone, whatsoever—not even himself. I think he took his eyes off of himself and he saw all those children running for cover. I think he suddenly realized that his life wasn't to be handed over so pointlessly, that in realizing how much harm he could do, he also realized how much *good* he could do. Only problem was, now it was too late to try. He wasn't willing to end it, but he couldn't stay there, either. So he ran away."

"That's a good theory. Say he actually did save your life—why do you think he did that?"

"Oh, man. Well, we don't know if he actually did."

"I know, but *supposing* he did. Hypothetically. Why would he follow you from the old man's house and bring you back to camp?"

"I honestly have no clue." I chewed my lip and smiled at her. "Maybe because he knew I was trying to save *him*."

From there we went down to the dock. Kids wrapped in towels trudged up the hill as we walked down. Poor Hannah perspired buckets in her business suit. She wiped her brow and brought her hair back and dried the pages of her notebook, which were damp and pudgy in the humid-ity. The lifeguard team was picking up leftover lifejackets from the ground and throwing away the afternoon's collection of socks, sopping shirts, and empty bags of sunflower seeds.

We stood on the dock and I pointed out the canoe rack and the shal-lows where Jordan had launched off, evading interception. Here, Hannah just took notes. She wrote a page after plopping down, not minding the algae marks that will surely imprint themselves on her rear end. She even slipped off her shoes and put her feet into the water as she wrote. She would look up, brow furrowed in the sunshine, and then attack the wet notebook.

"You swim here much?" she asked.

"A couple times a week, at least."

"It's really beautiful out here."

I shaded my eyes and scanned the familiar horizon, made alien when I imagined it upside down.

"Yes," I agreed. "It really is."

She craned her neck and shielded her own eyes when she asked, "So, you believe in God and all that, right? Since this is a Christian camp?"

"Yes, I believe in the God Personage."

"Do you think Jordan believed in God?"

"That's a good question. I'd guess he probably has some distant belief in a God figure, but I can't say he was a Christian."

"So Jenni, your boss—she doesn't hire Christians exclusively?"

"She usually does, but I guess she made an exception for Jordan."

"Why?"

"I think she just wanted to give him a chance to have this experience. She, and Jordan's mother, thought it might be good for him."

"Do you think it was?"

"Do I think it was what?"

"Good for him?"

"In its own way, maybe."

I sat a couple feet down from her, then she said, "I heard about what you did and just had to interview you. I've never met someone who spoke this kindly about a convict. It makes me want to ask if you forgive Jordan for what he did."

"Oh, I forgive him. Sure. We all do, I think. We all feel like we could've done more to help him, but yeah, we forgive him. We really hope he's all right."

Hannah let out a big breath and said, "Is there anything else you want to tell me about what happened? About Jordan?"

One small caveat about how no one was to blame for Jordan's gun-fire and escape—according to a cold form of calculus, *I* was to blame. I sincerely doubt Jordan would have rummaged through Jerry's house and turned the place upside down looking for a gun if I hadn't mentioned its whereabouts the night before. He got confused for old man Kyle on the hayride, sitting next to me in the darkness, and the idea hatched—maybe he *was* a form of old man Kyle, there to haunt the kids and baffle his fellow staffers. Maybe he was meant to become the legend that future employees and tenants would pine over and contemplate. "We never did find him," a future iteration of Hunter Saint would say on the trailer, a blank gleam of austerity in his eye. "To this day, you can hear him on the outskirts of camp, rowing a canoe up and down the channel, searching for the gun he left be-hind. And sometimes, if you swim out to the middle of the lake, an empty canoe will pass you by, and the figure of a man will appear on the dock, but if you try to crawl to land another way, he'll *follow* you, until you're forced to either swim to shore or drown."

I looked at Hannah, and said, "No. I don't think so."

July 20th

The story came out today. I printed it out in Jenni's office and read it before breakfast this morning:

The Mystery Behind Jordan Caol's Disappearance

A staffer at Camp Woodward describes his experience of weathering the elements in search of the 18-year-old man who fired a gun at Camp Woodward and then fled.

By Hannah Reardon

Hunter Saint walks with his head down, usually. At about six foot four and a slim, athletic build, he's an obvious candidate to work as a lifeguard in one of Oklahoma's remotest summer camps—Camp Woodward, where just a month ago, a young man named Jordan Caol fired a gun, harming no one, and consequently fled into the wilderness. He hasn't been sighted since by civilians or authorities.

Last week I visited Camp Woodward and spoke to Hunter Saint myself. His voice is gentle, and he speaks with a kind of self-deprecation, as if his word isn't quite enough to explain to me just the gravity of this "crazy" summer. Camp Woodward is located just a few miles north of Steuben, Oklahoma, and can only be reached by taking a lengthy gravel road that travels through fields, forests, and ranchland peppered with cattle and oil rigs. Its director is Jenni Mailer, and its staff stands at around a dozen, mostly college-aged students. While the camp is small, it hosts several church groups each summer. Pastors and youth leaders say they like Camp Woodward for its "off the charts" location and for the friendly staff. It's a nice spot. A thirty-acre lake spans the foot of the camp, surrounded by thick forest, and just from experience, I can tell you the star-count at night is utterly unmatched. Camp Woodward is a hidden gem, known by few, but which has now attracted statewide attention.

What isn't as well known is that a few days after Caol's disappearance, Saint embarked on a two-week journey from Adler all the way back up to the mouth of Lake Woodward in search of Caol. He took little with him besides the basics: a mountain-pack, a tent, sleeping bag, and a journal, which he's been writing in all summer as a part of a final class assignment for college. Saint followed the Green River, which flows out of Lake Woodward and runs only a few yards from his childhood home in Adler. "I just couldn't stop thinking about [Jordan]," he said. Saint wasn't interested in bringing Caol to justice. His mission was more pastoral. He wanted to find the escapee and encourage him to come back to Camp Woodward, face the consequences, but ultimately find redemption in Jesus Christ. Saint never found Caol. He did, however, find clues.

"I found the canoe he stole from camp," said Saint. "It was turned upside down in the river about twenty miles downstream from Lake Woodward. I also found both his shoes, although they were in different places. One was in the canoe, and another was in an abandoned stone building that was standing nearby. But ultimately, I met someone who had in fact encountered Jordan."

Saint described his bizarre encounter with someone simply referred to as "the old man," who initially held Saint at gunpoint in the woods before inviting him into his trailer house to have lunch. The old man, whom authorities can't seem to identify even upon investigation, claimed to Saint that Caol stayed with him for days, and had left the morning before.

"If that was true, then we had just missed each other," Saint said. "The old man said Jordan was traveling south towards the Oklahoma/ Texas border, while I was obviously going north."

The hardest point in the journey came when Saint left the old man's trailer house and had to decide if he was going to head south to try his luck again or go back to Camp Woodward. He decided to head back to camp, since he thought people would be worrying about him after two weeks of being gone. In fact, local authorities put out a "missing" alert for Saint, and a Facebook prayer group notched over 1,000 members strong shortly after he left for his mission. Saint also said that his decision to come back to camp represented "a kind of letting go," a realization that he wasn't going to find Jordan. At least, not yet.

What happened next remains a mystery, both for Saint and the entire Camp Woodward community. On an evening in late June, Saint appeared unconscious on the dock at Camp Woodward. By the time he was found, he'd been bitten by a water moccasin, a type of pit viper that's more venomous than a rattlesnake and even more aggressive. It also appeared that he'd suffered a semi-severe concussion. Saint remembers the snake, and he remembers hitting his head on a rock in the shallows when he fell from surprise.

The question is: who found him and brought him back to Camp Woodward?

Saint insists that he was a mile away from camp property when he was bitten and consequently struck his head on the rock. According to Lorrie Briggs, one of the camp staff members who found Saint, he was definitely brought back to camp by someone in a canoe. "I thought I saw someone rowing a canoe really fast into the channel," said Briggs. "But I didn't look too close, just because I was freaking out over Hunter, and I can't be sure who it was. It might have even been my imagination. Sometimes you think you see things out here that you really don't."

Briggs and Jerry Blankenship, a maintenance hand, took Saint to the nurse's station at Camp Woodward, where he was stabilized and given an IV due to dehydration. The medic noted that much of the venom in Saint's body had seemingly been withdrawn, indicating that someone did in fact discover him in the woods and orally extract snake venom while the bite was still fresh.

For Saint, there are really only two options—either the old man or Caol himself brought him back to safety. "In all honesty, we don't know," said Jenni Mailer, camp director. "We're just thankful to God that Hunter's okay. I honestly didn't care so much about how he got back than I did for the fact that he got back at all, if that makes sense. I don't think we could've handled him going missing as a staff. Not after what happened with Jordan."

Saint made a relatively quick recovery, and has returned to his normal work schedule at Camp Woodward. He showed me around the place last week, from the rec field where the incident occurred to the dock where he was later found unconscious.

"It's been a crazy summer to say the least," he said, looking out over the water and giving his trademark gentle smile. "I don't quite have the words for it. Not sure I ever will."

The search for Caol has lessened in the last couple of weeks, but a private investigator from Oklahoma City, Samuel Fratney, has been hired by the State to investigate the case further.

When I asked Saint what he took away from all of this, he was quiet for a long time. He looked tired, sad, even, as we sat on the dock speaking of the summer's tumultuous events.

"*The main thing I've taken away is a question,*" he said, still gazing into the distance.

"*What question?*" I asked him.

"*Why?*" he said. "*Why did God put us here, if he put us here at all? And whose fault is all this? I think that's what everyone's been asking.*"

"*You mean everyone at Camp Woodward?*"

He smiled and looked at me, then said, "*That. And everyone else in the world, too.*"

July 23rd

I went upstairs to the sound booth above the cafeteria after dinner for no particular reason except to peruse the shelf of Bibles that thirty summers' worth of kids have left behind. NIV Teen Study Bible. Belonged to Shana L. Too bad for Shana. Now her copy of God's word is cloistered between two King Jameses, along with about fifty leather-bound ESVs, which around here, people tend to call "extra-saved version." I'm the proud owner of a New American Standard Bible—the word for word translation, if you will. No one else I know touts around a New American. But it doesn't really matter. What matters, I guess, is that all these Bibles were left behind and shelved and now no one ever reads them, except for mice.

I did spot a book hiding at the very end of the shelf, though, and by its paper spine and comparatively thinner width, knew it wasn't the Holy Book butchered into English. I picked it up and held before me a title that by all means probably should have never been in a Protestant Baptist audio booth: *Introduction to the Devout Life,* by Francis de Sales. It was underlined to no end, almost on every page.

I slipped the book into my bag and shuffled off to the dorms. A storm is rolling in from the west and is projected to give us about two solid inches overnight. I'm free this evening, though, and so hunched up in the attic above the dorm and started reading old Francis, a fine old Catholic brother from the 1600s, and a fellow writer and monk in residence, it would seem.

July 24th

Last night, Zach and I took Jenni's mule down the trails way back into the woods behind the rec field, intertwining insofar as the trail would allow, until the jouncing vehicle chanced upon the lone carcass of a longhorn.

 I feel like we've both realized the tenuous future of having such experiences at Camp Woodward—the last camp comes and goes in less than two weeks. It's like earlier in the summer when I was already tuckered out and then feeling anxious about getting rest whenever we had an off day.

We stopped the mule and slipped out to investigate. The bull lay on its side, glassy eyes reflecting nothing of the great beyond, and one of its curled horns had snapped, probably from its fall, and lay like a distended arm next to its head. Zach wondered aloud how it had died. No predator had gutted its belly. It had acquired no stench. It was just a dead cow, conveniently splayed on our secret trail.

"There's no way we can move it," I said, nudging it with my boot. "I bet Jerry would want to see this."

"Jerry would want to burn it. That's what Jerry'd want to do," said Zach. He bent down, the mule humming behind us, and clucked his tongue. "Dad gum," he said.

You expect the carcasses of coyotes, possums, and armadillos on such excursions. For some reason a longhorn doesn't fit the bill, though.

"Who does he belong to?" I asked.

Zach checked the ear. It was engraved with an C with a fencepost running through it. "Caol Ranch," he said.

"Beg your pardon."

"That's the name of the ranch ten miles south. I recognize the emblem. This bugger escaped his brood."

"You say Caol Ranch."

"Yeah. Haven't you seen it before?"

"Can't say that I have." Realizing my friend had missed the obvious, I said, "Any relation to *Jordan* Caol, do you think?"

"No way," said Zach. Then he paused. He checked the branded lettering again and then stepped away, frowning.

"That is weird, though," he said. "Maybe it's the same family. Distant kin? I thought he lived with his mom."

"He did. Apparently. Although I never saw her. Did you?"

"No. Did no one think to check the ranch with his namesake plastered on the entry gate?"

"It's probably a coincidence."

"Coincidence." Zach shook his hand. "Man, brother, I don't mind telling you this, but this whole summer is starting to give me the creeps."

"I get that."

Caol Ranch was just the name of a ranch. Jordan was no son of a rancher. He was somebody's son, but not of a rancher. His father, if he still had one, sojourned somewhere in Texas. "What's it all mean, buddy," said Zach. "God trying to tell us something, or what?"

We turned around to return to camp and were mostly quiet on the way back. I didn't ask him about his relationship with Carli. It's so hard to talk about that kind of stuff with Zach. Far as Lorrie and I could tell they'd accumulated some newfound distance since the carnival escapade on the tomahawk ride. I glanced at him as he drove, the light from the headlights revealing enough to make out his ever-working jaw, betraying his Stoicism, and the half-mad concentration in his eyes suggesting he was holing up his entire life behind their lenses. You can't hide from your friends. Not your real ones.

Zach has no idea what he wants to do with his life. He was a sociology major in college and put off thinking about his future at the altar of the football. But college is over. As we drove away from that dead cow, it really hit me. College is over, and so, on an impending basis, is Camp Woodward.

We parked the mule outside of Jenni's and slipped inside her house. She was arranging a line of cups of tea for her precursing guests: Lorrie, Carli, and Gabbie, who sprawled on the L-shaped couch in the living room in various shapes that accorded with their level of exhaustion. Lorrie slid half-unconsciously to the rug, corpse-like, and snored.

"It's that time of the summer," said Jenni. Zach and I sat down at her countertop. "Zombie season."

"We found a dead longhorn," said Zach. "It was just laying there on the trail about two miles away."

"Well, did you hit it with the mule?"

I notified her that no, we weren't the culprits here.

"Things die," said Jenni. "Even big old bulls." She slid us a pair of mugs and asked us what kind of tea we wanted.

"Honey lemon sounds good."

"I don't want any," said Zach, taking off his hat. He spun in his chair to face the dim living room.

After I supped on the tea and Jenni fluttered away to clean something obscure, it was 11 p.m. and zombie-ness descended on me too. I drank and breathed deep breaths through my nose, as if this might keep my eyelids from drooping. Zach fidgeted at the door. I put the mug into the sink. I wanted to ask him how he was doing. We haven't really talked all summer. You know how it goes, Professor Snodgrass. Guys don't like to talk about their feelings, but the secret's out: they all want to, deep down. Or need to at times, rather. It takes little more than three months of chaos and suspended communication to bury a friendship for good, turns out. You gotta talk. Get the sentences flowing. Wordless trips in the mule can't reignite the bond, either. But I didn't say anything on our walk back to the dorms. The locusts seemed louder even than the engine of the mule, lulled me like the sirens calling out in the Aegean, and we both ebbed into the darkness of the dorm rooms once we got back, with no lights to carve passage, and crawled into slumber with a muffled, "G'night, bro," and nothing else.

Am I thinking about dying too much? Falling asleep in darkness after patting a dead bull's broken horn doesn't help with the death dread, though. That and, of course, almost dying yourself. Yes. Things definitely die. People, cows, friendships.

But this summer can't die. It can't end. Not yet.

Jerry just walked into the cafeteria to help wash the morning dishes. He's wearing his pistol, the one his dead grandfather gave him, in a holster of cowboy leather on his hip.

July 30th

Checked the boy's dorms, the bathrooms in the game room (somehow clean) lifeguarded at the waterfront, torn between protecting the lives of the swimming children minnows and watching Lorrie swing her legs and support herself with her tan arms, chewing her whistle. She smiles when she knows I'm watching her.

Following dinner, after the kitchen was mopped and the girls scuttled off to Jenni's for their weekly Bible study, I followed Jerry down to the lake at a distance. He carried a Shakespeare fishing rod, smoked a cigarette, and still carried the pistol on his hip. Shooting fish wasn't beyond him. A shotgun might behoove that method of sport more fittingly, but he'd depend on the rod first. He didn't hear me come up on him. Country music, a Toby Keith-er from the twang of it, yawled from his pocket. I stood about thirty feet behind him, barefoot in the grass and almost turned back around. The summer was almost over. I wasn't sure if it was worth it. Nope. Back around, forward, head up.

"Hey Jerry," I said. He glanced behind his shoulder, lifting the flat bill of his hat so he could see who I was, and then said, "Hey bud. What are you doin' down here?" He blew smoke through his nostrils and fitted the pole between his legs, impaling a worm on the hook.

"I come down here after dinner sometimes," I said. True enough.

"You ever fish here?"

"Nah. I don't know why, though. Dad and I fly fish a lot on the Green in our spare time."

"Yeah? I've gotten into fly fishing in the last couple years."

"We'll have to go sometime."

He let the bait swing out as he brandished the rod, leaned it back, and tossed the bait into the water. He reeled slowly, ash falling like snow on the copper whiskers of his chin, his rabid green eyes catching sunshine. He turned down the country music but didn't shut it off. For a minute or so I just stood there. It was so awkward. I had to put my hands in my pockets and scuff the edge of the dock with my big toe and pretend that it was normal for Jerry and me to talk like this after a complete summer of not speaking a word.

The end of Jerry's pole tartly bent, then stilled. He held his breath and tried to hook it but missed the lip. Then without looking at me he said, "You got something to talk to me about, Saint?"

"I do, actually," I said. "I've been meaning to talk to you pretty much all summer."

"You gave us a pretty good scare there in June," he said. "I went out hiking a few times trying to find you. Hunt you down."

"Sorry about that."

"It ain't a big deal. I shot four coyotes while I was out there."

"With that pistol?" I pointed at the weapon in question. He nodded but didn't say anything back.

"Yeah, it was a crazy time. Crazy time." Nothing I haven't said before.

"Well, what'd you have to say?"

He cast to the right side of the dock on the cusp of some cattails, from which a fat water moccasin, disturbed from the meteoric worm, shot out and slithered ashore. Jerry said, "Shit!" And then he set the fishing rod on the dock and drew the pistol, cocking, aiming, and holding the gun forth with his right arm extended and his left fingering the empty holster. The bullet blew the moccasin's head off when he shot it. It snapped off, in fact, like a faucet designed to gush blood, flying into the reeds. We hustled over to the body as it writhed under the punishment of its post-mortem nervous system. It jiggled its way back into the shallows, thrashing, and then floated backside up.

"Nice shot!"

"Thanks. Freakin' water moccasins." He stamped the cigarette beneath his boot and added, "Can't believe you got bit by one, man."

We went back to the dock and I had to try and start all over again. Only problem was that Jerry's pole was swimming east across the lake and downward, led doubtlessly by one of the biggest catfish in Lake Woodward. Jerry cussed again, and we watched the rod duck underwater twenty yards out, bob up for a moment's reprieve, and then spin in circles like some zany version of roulette. By the time the monster snapped the line, the pole floated and pointed down the channel.

"I can get it," I said.

"Nah, dude, don't worry about it. It's not my only pole."

"Forget it, man, I'm in shorts. It won't take but a minute."

I took off my shirt and dove from the dock, swimming underwater with my eyes closed, and came up with the rod only barely in view. It was farther out than I originally thought, right in the middle of the lake. By the time I reached it, the sun had fallen below the tops of the trees. I snatched the rod and made the return voyage swimming on my back.

I was maybe about twenty feet away from the dock when I could detect Jerry's upside down form on the periphery. He was holding the pistol at his hip and looking at his phone in the other. From my newly preferred upside-down worldview, he was pointing the gun at the sky, a.k.a. the lake, a.k.a. the looking glass of murk and mystery that you can't truly peer through until you dive into it.

"Thanks man," he said. "I shouldn't have left it like that on the dock."

"No worries." I handed the thing up to him and pulled myself up.

"All right," he said. "What'd you have to say to me?"

I let myself catch my breath. I wrung my ears out and mopped my face with my shirt. Then I told him. Without beating around the bush. Straight as an arrow. Taut as a fishing line. I told him that Jordan knew where his grandfather's gun was because I told him on the night of the legend of old man Kyle, and that the unfortunate events of the summer, when measured through simple cause and effect mathematics, were my fault. Jerry looked at the water. His jaw worked and his green eyes narrowed in the same kind of pain Jenni and I saw him the night he busted the water pipe.

"I'm sorry, man," I said after I was done. "I was trying to talk to him on that hayride. Make conversation. I never thought anything of it."

"It's not your fault." Jerry wiped his nose and continued, "I usually lock my door every day, but I was so pissed off about the water pipe feelin' like I can't do one damn thing right around here that I kicked the door off its hinges. I fixed it that night, but by then the gun was gone. Nothin' else disturbed in the whole house, which was the weird part. But nah, man. Don't blame yourself. If there's anybody to blame it's me."

I had expected a few different outcomes out of this exchange, such as Jerry wrangling me by the haunches and sending me soundly into the iono-sphere, but passing the buck to himself wasn't on the list. We clapped hands and brought it in for a bro hug, and then faced the lake together with our arms crossed. Jerry took out the pistol and laughed to himself. "Anyway," he said. "We could go on about this forever. Maybe we were a bit careless, but Jordan chose to fire the gun, and he chose to leave, too. Sometimes there ain't nothing you can do about it."

"That's true."

I sighed, and we watched, out of the impending darkness, a wooden canoe drift unmanned across the center of the lake. We didn't say anything. We just watched it. It wasn't uncommon after floods for driftwood and dead animals to float by. Treasure can pop up amid the flotsam. It had rained two nights before, so maybe that drudged it up from one of the creeks or narrow channels unbeknownst to our mental maps. All the way from the old man's house.

"The lost canoe returns," said Jerry.

After a pause he added, "Who's old man Kyle, you think? In that story you were telling on the hayride. I always wondered where that story came from."

"I don't know," I said. "Far as I can tell, if we're talking figuratively or whatever, he's either one of two Personages: Death or God. If we want to get all mythic, you know."

"Dang. I hope he's God. I think."

"Yeah. Me too."

The canoe floated to the opposite shore. Only, in this iteration of the ghost story scene, there were two figures on the dock instead of just one, and there was no struggling swimmer in the middle of the lake.

August 1st

Last night, I was given the honor of conducting what turned out to be the last hayride of the summer. I hadn't done it since June, when Jordan was with me to hear the tale of old man Kyle, and it wasn't until clambering upon the helm of the trailer that it felt so eerie to be up there, and with twenty twelve-year-olds whispering on the haybales below me. As Jerry started up the tractor and we rumbled towards the trail, they started asking for a ghost story.

"You don't want to hear a ghost story—too scary!" I shouted.

"Aw c'mon!"

"I don't know...I think we'd need to get written slips of permission from your parents, and that would take hours."

"Aw c'mon!"

A burly young fellow with stickiness on his cheeks went on the offensive and blurted, "You just don't *know* any ghost stories!"

"Now *that* couldn't be further from the truth," I said. I was sweating. A bump in the road dislocated my balance, made me feel queasy when I pulled myself upright again.

"Aw c'monnnn!"

So I conceded, setting up the ghost story about Old Man Kyle, when from beyond the trailer I *swear* I saw a slender humanoid figure walking behind us on the rocky trail. It was only for a second, and then the back lights of the tractor moved on to shine on closer real estate, but it was as evident as day for the second it lasted and had me tongue tied in my seat.

"Well, mister?" said our pugnacious boy from Tahlequah.

"We're almost back to camp," I said. "I don't have time to tell you this story right now. It's too long. Too complicated...too scary."

Fortunately, an argument broke out about who was better: Russell Westbrook or Kevin Durant—a heated debate flummoxed by prejudice and emotion among Oklahomans.

When we rolled back to the party barn, the kids dismounted and I went up to the tractor to have a word with Jerry.

"That was the last one I'm doing tonight," he said, turning off the ignition.

"All right. I think I dropped my hat on the trail. I'm gonna go loop around once to go check.

130

"Okay."

I trotted down the gravel road until reaching the trailhead at the foot of the trees, and then stopped, listening for a moment to the chatter of kids in the party barn and the breeze blowing down from the northwest. Another storm was coming.

I didn't have my phone with me, of course, but took out a small keychain flashlight and brandished it with one hand as I ventured into the darkness.

There was no light under the trees. I had to step carefully to avoid ankle breaking stones and ruts in the trail, but managed it all right, shining the flashlight in front of me and trying not to wonder, to hope.

There's no question about it. Someone was following the hayride and was lurking around in the woods.

I started panicking a little bit, feeling like I should've brought Zach and Jerry along with me after telling them what I saw, but I didn't go back. I walked up and down the gulley, came briefly into the back rec field, and then snaked back into the forest for the second half of the loop. Stratus clouds decorated the sky, fizzed with distant lightning. The wind, at least for a second, was chilly.

I shone my flashlight through the trees and even up into the branches, breathing shallow, walking faster with every step and regretting myself. But there wasn't any doubt about seeing *something*. In any case, I just had to make sure.

I was probably about halfway through the second part of the loop, nearing the sandy road that connects to the waterfront, when the leaves rustled to my right, a human being stood to length, and spoke in a whisper, "Hunter."

I scuttled down the trail, slipping and falling, then flipped on my chest and snatched the flashlight. Whoever it was came out of the trees now and stood on the trail behind me. I scrambled to my feet and let the beam fall where it would, right upon the pale face of Jordan Caol.

"Hunter, it's me."

"Holy Jesus."

Jordan swallowed and fidgeted in his steps. He wore work boots and a flannel shirt, and his hair was tied back in a ponytail. He'd even grown wisps of a beard on his lip and cheeks.

For about thirty seconds, maybe more, I just shone the light on his face while he blinked, perhaps understanding my shock, and said nothing. Then he shaded his eyes and said, "Didn't mean to scare you."

"Jordan. Dude—what…what are you doing here? How long have you been here?"

"I never really left," he said, shrugging.

"Come again?"

"I didn't go far."

"Okay…"

I realized then that I had one foot forward, knee bent, and my fingers bent like cat claws.

"I don't want to hurt you," said Jordan.

I straightened up, and then hung the flashlight on a branch near my head.

"I'm guessing you've been staying with that old man?"

He nodded. He crossed his arms and stayed silent.

"The whole time?"

"Pretty much, yeah."

"So you were there when I was."

He shrugged again. I could see his shoulders go up-down against the stars behind him, and a strike of distant lightning light up his languid gray eyes. And then there was the silence again. Building up between us, two whole months' worth. He said nothing to me and I said nothing to him. We just listened to the thunder roll and the locusts amp up their chatter, until finally I said, "You gotta come back with me."

"I can't do that, man."

"Sure you can. We're at the edge of camp. You don't have to run anymore. You don't have to hide. It's okay. It's all right."

"Nah." He cleared his throat. "I got nowhere to go. That probably sounds exaggerated, but you have no idea—there is *no* place I can go."

"That's not true."

"If I go to camp, I go to jail. You know that."

He wasn't wrong.

"We'll figure it out. You're not alone, man."

"Yes, I am. But it's okay. It's okay."

"Nothing's going to be solved if you walk away."

"I'm not coming back."

"So why are you here now?"

"I wanted to say goodbye. I shouldn't have done what I did, but that's over for me now, and I gotta live with it. You were basically the only person who talked to me when I was at camp, and I wanted to talk more. It probably didn't seem like it, but I did." He kept glancing away and kicking at the rocks with his boot. He shoved his hands in his pockets so his shoulders looked like they were in a perpetual shrug.

"I wanted to talk to you more, too, man." At that point, the obvious question resurged in my mind, but Jordan was backing away now, clearing his throat again and inching into the woods.

"Wait a minute."

He waited.

"I gotta know. Did you pull me in that day when I hit my head on the log?"

Jordan didn't answer. He held something out in in the palm of his hand instead, only barely discernible in the shadows, and waited. It was only when I took it from him, with some hesitation, that I recognized the cold steel surface of the pistol I'd packed the day I set out to look for him.

"I'll see ya, Hunter," he mumbled. "And I'm sorry I didn't give up my phone. You were just trying to help me." He looked toward camp, then back at me, then turned around into the night.

He crunched through the leaves, headed to the lakeside after I whispered after him to no avail. I ran to the dock. He paddled out into the channel in a canoe out of a tiny inlet where the deer went to drink, a moot point against the water, and then disappeared as I debated whether to chunk the spare canoe in the water and go after him yet again. By I just stood there on the dock, breathing hard, clutching the pistol.

Back at camp, the crew was breaking down the inflatables at the party barn. Jenni barked orders and the last of the campers glided back to their dorms. I showed up, all pale-faced and speechless, and Jenni came up and slapped me on the shoulder. "Where've you been?"

I looked at her for a few seconds as if trying to remember who she was, then snapped out of it and said, "Had to go look for something I lost."

"Did you find it?" she asked.

I gave her my half smile that usually doesn't convince. "Yeah. I did."

It was only until getting back to the dorms that I realized I was still holding the gun, covered by a sleeve. It was cocked and loaded, though not from my doing, and my finger was resting on the trigger.

I don't think I'll ever see Jordan Caol again.

August 7th

Last full day at Camp Woodward. Got most of my stuff packed up this morning. I almost forgot to go up to the attic above the boys' dorm and sit at the elementary school desk in front of the box fan. Hot as ever up there. But as bright as it was in the midmorning sun, I couldn't help, as felt fitting, slouching in the brilliance and turning my face to the glass and get slammed with light. Is this what old Francis witnessed after his scribblings and devotions? Unbearable lightness? Both of spirit and of being?

I swept the desk free of dust, kicked the beanie bag out of the way, and slipped through the trapdoor unsure if I'd ever trespass into the little nook ever again.

There's been the usual sessions of communal selfies among the gals, teary embraces, and recursions of inside jokes. The rookies are now Woodward converts. The legacy seems to be secure. But it's time for the veterans to bow out and move on.

Mom and Dad told me something the other night over the phone that I've dismissed as of late. They said I used to write everything down after any kind of trip we took. Can you believe that, Professor Snodgrass? I used to write stuff down after junior high basketball games, the highs and the lows of my performance. I used to log the mundane events of schooldays like they were war ledgers. She said, "Don't you remember when you'd go out into the woods and describe all the trees? You'd go out looking for mushrooms and beetles and birds and copperheads and water moccasins and weird toads? And remember how you loved *bees* especially? The way they buzzed and honeyed and combed their lives away? Don't you remember that you wanted so badly to *keep* everything in words as under a lock and key?"

I hadn't forgotten. Maybe it was just sort of painful to realize I'd largely parted ways with my childlike wonder. In college, all my attention was aimed at the textbook and through the microscope. There's nothing wrong with that at all, and you have to do it. But you can get lost in the bureaucracy of the science lab, lose the confrontation of the praying mantis and the tiger orange velvet on the back of a Monarch butterfly. You can lose that when you stop keeping a handbook and an open eye.

We're always trying to force things, aren't we? You started shooting hoops in the driveway, giggling with the delight of the ball's arc and its swoosh through the net, to waking up one morning and feeling like if you don't make the NBA your life is worth diddily squat. Or you splashed finger paint on a canvas in pre-school and your eyes were fixed like fiery planets on those meaningless, meaning-filled creations. Then you wake up ten years yonder and find that it takes profound squinting and internal resistance just to appreciate a simple sunset that's not yet subdued and pixelated by your iPhone 39 X Pro Nifty Gifty Hoppity Zoppity Do Dang-er. You used to catalog walking sticks in the backyard and then you're sticking them into tubes to draw their DNA.

In a sense, it's true I haven't kept a real journal until this summer. Those days my mom mentioned were about logging the things I saw. Things that just happened. Was there a story in those ledgers? I guess at some point the most analytical fellow out there has to take a stab at self-knowledge. It feels like doing surgery on yourself, probing the heart depths and seeing what dredge and fine wine will spring up. Some days it feels like a merry go round, leading nowhere. Like none another than a grinning tomahawk going in circles mainly for the sake of circulating. What's the point? That none of us, and perhaps me most of all, are as mysterious as we assume? That we really do all share the same hopes and fears and bigotries and shortcomings? We write in our journals and have our mental soliloquies. Suppose that's a joint chorus, in the end?

Well, here we are at the last page. Sitting here with Zach at the end of the summer staff dinner. Lorrie and Carli are laughing over their barbecue. Yes, we're dating, by the way, Professor Snodgrass. Knew you'd just be *dying* to know. There was no way not to take the plunge. We've got nothing left to fake anymore. We'll take it slow but mark my words—we won't be awkwardly shuffling around at this year's Christmas Party, avoiding each other like second cousins. Jenni is whittling her tooth by the kitchen with a toothpick, smiling to herself.

Last night, I was on water and trash duty, and near midnight, drove the mule to the water jug under the canopy that stands in the middle of the rec field. There, I took a long drink from the plastic waterspout. Then, I just sat at the empty picnic table under the canopy, wet and tired, with Camp Woodward before me glowing under its orange street lights like Nineveh. I was on the border there. Wilderness behind, order before. Teetering on the narrow way that only the unbalanced can traverse.

I sat there for a long time. Not sure how long. An hour, maybe. Completely wordless. Phoneless. The universe shining and smiling overhead. It was weird, not knowing if I'd ever be sitting there again. Lorrie walked over after a while and asked if she could join me from a few feet away. "Please." She sat down on the table and leaned her head against my shoulder and turned her own eyes to the stars.

"Are you all right?" she said.

"I think so. Just trying to soak it all in."

She sighed. "Yeah. Me too."

"I saw Jordan."

The words came out of my mouth, and I couldn't put them back in. It was like someone roped the syllables in my lungs and yanked. She lifted her head and faced me.

"You...*saw* him?"

I nodded, surprised at my own calmness. "Yeah. The night of the last haybale ride." I told her the whole story, how I'd brought along a pistol with me from home only to find it missing when I showed up on the dock. How he gave the pistol back to me. How he could have killed me and hurt all those kids on the hayride but didn't. How that didn't change what he'd done back in June but maybe it did.

"What are you going to do?"

I shook my head. "I almost followed him in one of the boats. But I don't know. Something held me back. And I don't want to tell the cops, or Jenni. Maybe I should. It just felt like..."

"Like what?"

"Like that was his way of saying he was never coming back." I looked at her. "He's not going to hurt anybody."

"That's what you always believed."

"Yeah. I just hope he finds what he's looking for."

"You saw him. I can't believe it."

"I haven't told anybody else."

We half-expected Jordan to come out of the darkness and sit down next to us. Nothing but a coyote though, ranging for food, darted across the field and ran into the trees.

Later on, past midnight, I took my tent and sleeping bag and set up camp on the dock. I laid on my back and watched the cosmos flywheel through the mesh, thinking, trying to land on a big takeaway.

I'll just say this: I was waiting for someone to come out of the woodwork to tell me really important things about the world, in however outback a dialect. Someone to teach me the narrow way of the channel less traveled.

Which tempting streams, in turn, to abjure. For the sake of the narrative, Prof, let's just say I was waiting for old man Kyle. And I think he showed up, eventually, calling from somewhere deep in the forest, from somewhere infinite among the stars, from somewhere minuscule beneath my bare feet, from somewhere hidden in the cracks of the past three months. Hunting in the darkness. Standing on the dock, waiting for the lost kid to swim back home.

This morning, early birds chattered in the trees and the canoe wasn't on the other side of the lake anymore when I rolled over to peek at the sunrise. I just lay there in the warm dewiness wondering how this summer went by so fast. It's like I came down to the dock with this creative writing assignment, fell asleep, and just woke up with the whole thing already done on my lap.

All I know right now is that my last summer at Camp Woodward is over, but we're still here. How amazing that anyone is here at all! I wonder if this generation of Camp Woodward will always be here, in a sense, waiting for the lost boy in the canoe to float back to the dock, whether that's me, Jordan, Zach, or the whole busted-up world searching for the nurse's station.

I was about halfway up the sandy road when Jenni came out of one of the little cabins on the edge of the trees and plopped a bunch of laundry on the porch. I stopped and waited for her. She walked over while Lorrie and Zach showed up at the end of the road, also approaching me, side by side. I didn't know what was going on when Jenni snapped her fingers, held out her hand, and said, "Let me carry the tent, or whatever that is." I didn't know why Zach, without a word, took the mountain pack off my back, or why Lorrie held my hand in hers.

"Why are you carrying all this?" said Jenni. I don't think she was talking about the tent and the mountain pack.

"I don't know."

"Look at me."

I looked at her and away from the ground. She put her hand on my shoulder and smiled.

"You don't have to carry it all, Hunter. Okay?"

"Okay. Yeah. Okay, Jenni."

And we walked up the hill together.

There you have it, Professor Snodgrass. That's about all I got in me. If you want a short version of the story, here it is: Hunter Saint got saved this summer.

September 3rd, 2017, 3:49 P.M.

P.S:

Dear Professor Snodgrass,

Just a final note, if you're interested: I walked back out to that trailer house just to see if the old man was still living out there, and if Jordan might still be there, too. That was on August 10th after everyone else had already driven home and Jenni was sleeping off the summer. But when I reached what I was sure to be the right spot, all that was there was that ancient rusty plough, mostly overgrown with brambles, pointing towards Texas. The rest of the property must have been washed away in the late summer floods. I stayed the night out there, listening to the sounds of a dying summer—watching the stars that were watching me. Watching the world as seen through the eye of Old Man Kyle.